Partners Even When We Dance

Mo Lily

ISBN-13: 978-1484154014
ISBN–10: 1484154010

For Loo

And

Carol
Patsy
Joyce
Joan
Anita
Sandy
Hilda
Pat
Dolly
Maureen
Joan
Pat
Glynis
Trixie
Pat

And
Lil

I have danced with you all

If ego can ego mos
If I can I will

*To be fond of dancing was a certain
step towards falling in love*

Jane Austen

Chapter One

Forward, forward, back and side, it was simple. It was simple surely. One-step, two steps back then side. Nevertheless, what a muddle they got in.

'No Sandra side as in out, don't cross your feet dear.' Bang went the door.

Jean was taking her six o'clock dancing class for the hard to understand group, difficulty in learning or,

'Just right dopey' Grace her partner commented 'they will never learn, it is far too difficult, some of them have trouble walking.'

'Who banged that door? Was it someone coming or going?'

'It was George he has gone'

'Oh gone, home, or will he be back? Did he say goodbye to any of us?'

'No idea I haven't heard him say a word

since he arrived, paid his two pounds and just sat there.'

'Another one who can't do the side bit' said Sandra. Clapping her hands Jean put a stop to what they were doing.

'Right, now we are going to do the samba' she said with excitement.

'Oh goody' came from her pupils.

'This'll be a laugh' said Grace.

'I wish you would keep your comments to yourself and be a bit more useful.'

Talking loud and slowly with a huge smile Jean told them,

'Grace is going to help us with this'

'Oh heck, am I?'

'Yes dear'

'I'll be the man, I'm not dancing with Tommy Albright he makes grabs at your body parts when you get close'

'It's the samba love, arms-length away from each other.'

Rushing up to the stage end of the dance hall, she told her pupils

'I will put some music on then you can hear the jolly music, hum along to it, it will give you an idea of the rhythm then we will learn the steps.' Bang went the door again.

'Who is it now?' she was leaning round the side of the stage to try to see who it was.

'It's George back.' George came in looking at everyone he was licking an ice cream cone.

'Oh George look dear it does clearly say no food in here. If I let you eat that they will all want one, please go into the porch until it's gone' he slowly turned still licking.

'I want a fag' said Mary and she joined him in the porch.

'Right now where were we? Everyone got your partners? La, la-la - La, la-la' she sang along to the music, 'easy, listen to the timing. Now Grace come here, watch us everyone.' She grabbed hold of Grace who was not expecting it and stumbled forward laughing.

'One, one-two. One, one-two.' They gave a smooth demonstration of the samba to the music for a few minutes.

Turning the music off Jean and Grace received a little clap and a titter.

'Now it's your turn, down that end Grace.' Jean stood with her back to her pupils and very slowly went through the samba steps again for them to follow.

They tried to follow, only one or two

grasped the first step the one-two was baffling.

'ONE, one-two' she shouted emphasizing the One as she took a large step, looking nothing like the demonstration they gave.

Grace was trying to pull Connie's other leg backwards as she said she could not move.

For a quarter of an hour, this went on.

George and Mary came back and joined in giggling so much Jean wondered what they had been smoking.

'Now we will try the music, you may have to speed it up a bit.' A bit was not the right word to use. The music was jolly and rushing away with itself. Everyone was useless.

ONE, one-two, Jean shouted over the music.

'I can't do this' Pauline said and slumped down in a chair.

'Neither can I' said Trevor joining her.

'Oh dear forget the music for a while' she turned it off.

'When are we going to do the tango?' asked Tommy.

'Not yet dear that is really difficult'

'What do you want to do that for then?' asked Pauline.

'Because that's nice and cosy' said Tommy.

She gave him a sick look.

The clock struck the hour, immediately they all grabbed their coats, and two of them called out 'bye' others just left.

'Oh my' Jean sighed 'ten of them two pounds each that twenty quid and hour, less the rent for the hall'

'And half for me' said Grace.

'You must be joking. I'll give you a fiver.'

They slowly cleared up surprising how much mess they made in just an hour.

'A crisp packet, I missed that who was eating crisps, leave that around the verger will go mental.'

Jean hired a small church hall for her dancing lessons, paid by the hour, no heating as that was extra, but she considered if they danced hard enough they would not get cold probably the reverse and she would have to open the doors, letting her money out.

All clean and tidy, lights off, doors secure after locking up she had to return the key to the verger. At one time, she asked for a key of her own but he refused, she offered to get a new one cut and paid for but no, she might stay longer than the hour she had booked.

'If everyone did that then they would all be overlapping each other's times.' She was the only person who used the rotten damp place the cubs had long given up on it.

There was a time when a marching band thought it would be good for them as there were so many times they could not practice outside in bad weather.

'No' Jean told the verger 'have you seen the state of that floor, they will march right through it.' He explained this to the band they decided against it, they would look for somewhere with a concrete floor. She remained the only person to hire the place on a regular basis, and only because it was cheap.

Jean and Grace returned the key and went home. They lived together, lived as lesbian friends.

'I'm not a lesbian, for Christ sake I've got a child' Grace told Jean.

She indeed has a child, an adult child she rarely sees. She was married to Jeremy for eighteen, long years, mostly unhappy years, though at the time she was not aware of that.

A few years were nice, the early years, when her baby was young.

Her child was a girl, as stuck up as her father they lived in the Cotswolds, England.

That just about says it all for if there was one thing that Grace was not and did not know how to be, was stuck up.

Jean on the other hand would have liked the chance to be stuck up she would have made a good job of it. Her life had always been a downhill struggle.

Jean also had a child, two in fact, boys. Both married but living close to her, as also did her ex-husband. He lived very near and often called in to see them. Still loving Jean, and would take her back like a shot. He never has doubt that one day she will come back to him. Apart from what she took, everything at his home is the same as when she lived there.

He has never moved or touched anything. Never sleeps on her side of the bed keeps to his side religiously, as if she was still there.

The breakdown of their marriage was due to the fact he never did anything. Did not work, did not cook, and did not talk much. Certainly did not keep clean, always looked unkempt.

With the effort he tried to make now, it still did not work and he managed to look the same, scruffy and dirty, tramp like.

Jean used to leave him "To Do" lists and what a muck up he made of those instructions, if he read the note at all, he most often read it wrong, sometimes disastrously, like don't forget to feed the cat, it would come across as don't feed the cat. Poor pussy would be ravenous time Jean got home.

Jean is a schoolteacher, she teaches music and movement in a local town primary school. Teaching first year schoolchildren, who she had to admit most, were far better than her six o'clock class. She lived with Grace out of town, keeping their relationship private.

She was also the deputy head, with a headship impending. The now, head teacher Miss Collingwood was suffering badly from arthritis and ageing fast.

'Be glad to go' she repeatedly made that clear to all. It was an easy job, a nice school, nice kids and best of all, nice parents, Jean never had any problems.

Grace was an administrator at the town hall.

'Sounds impressive don't it? I do admin in that large building at the top of the high street with all those steps that I climb every day.'

'Good job you do dear that is the only exercise you get all day' as Jean always told her when she went on about those steps.

Jean worked fewer hours than Grace but left for school earlier, leaving first, she often still left "To Do" notes for Grace, who always managed a rude comment and very seldom did the request.

'I don't know why I bother' said Jean after leaving a job list which included putting out the very full dustbin before she left as Jean was running late. She came home to "Stuff it" written across her note and a still, full dustbin.

'I certainly don't know why you bother' came from Grace not at all concerned. Jean would be the one to make a trip to the rubbish tip before the week was out.

Coming home from work Grace was noticeably irritable and exhausted. Exhausted, sitting at a desk all day were Jean's thoughts.

'What's up love, is it that Brady again?' Jean asked giving her the sympathy she really did not feel towards her and the Mr Brady battle.

'Yes useless fucker thinks he can count, all he can count is how many cups of coffee I drink each day'

'I thought you could have a coffee when you wanted, as long as you drank it at your desk' thinking of the times during a class she would love a cup of coffee.

'I am but he counts them, tells me every sip I take I stop work. He will count the sips next.' Realising it was not just her coffee habit.

'Something else was it?'

'Yes he moved my desk'

'Oh how far did he move it?'

'Into another office, a small dingy cupboard of an office, with a window like a prison cell and I've seen bigger radiators in a pigeon's loft.' Jean gave a titter did they have radiators in pigeon lofts?

She felt sure Grace had never been inside a pigeon loft and most unlikely that she would not as much take look inside one.

'I told him I just needed a different desk with a modesty panel, oh no they do not have another desk, but another office, yes.'

'What difference would another desk make, I don't get it?'

'He said I sit with my legs open on purpose

and I don't wear underwear. What an imagination he's got, I nearly yanked me skirt up and showed him me draws.'

'He fancies you.'

'I think he got the message and doesn't fancy me any longer, I told you at the Christmas party when he came on strong and I rubbed his 'monies worth' for him, he was enjoying it until I got vicious and had a good tug. Physically sick he was all those mince pies he ate came up.'

'Counting them was you?'

'No I wasn't, just noticed he was nonstop, eating far more than anyone else.'

'Tea's ready, ham salad' said Jean as she put a plate of food in front of Grace.

'Boring' she said after taking a good look at the plate, but started tucking in just the same.

Chapter Two

Jean and Grace lived in an old Victorian terraced house the type that at one time had an outside toilet, and probably no bathroom.

With conversions, magnolia paint and all mod cons they were in demand. Still no garages, there were so many cars squashed outside each house, like themselves mostly two per household.

'Then if one did have a garage' Angela from next door was ready to note for you 'one rarely puts your car in it, and the garages were always full of junk.'

'Speak for yourself, we don't have junk.'

'But we could if we had a garage.'

Angela lived next door with Ron, but she said she lived with Ronald. Everyone else knew him as Ron. The other side lived Auntie Agnes she did not move next to them, they moved next to her.

Jean's mother's eldest sister, Aunt Agnes, approaching eighty or could be ninety, if not that already, no one could be sure, she told so many lies and never disclosed her correct age, she liked to think she was seventy something.

On one of their often visits to Auntie they see the "For Sale" sign outside the house next door. Agnes was in a right state about the builders who put in the mod cons, then she had a huge concern who would buy it, how many kids, motorbikes or dogs they would have. Discovering the asking price, she said it would never sell, so she was not worried anymore.

Jean had always liked this road and he surrounding area, Grace agreed and moving next door to Auntie would be delightful not a problem. She never knew until moving day that they had bought the place.

'Moving in they are, Friday, new neighbours, that is my peace gone, one maybe its two dogs and a cat to crap in my garden, never use their own you know,' she told them.
'Where does she get her information from?'

'I think it's her home help, she may have said hope they haven't got dogs or a cat and Auntie believes it is definite.'

'Wonder how many kids she's got us down for then?'

Auntie sat in her chair in front of her television and did not move much, so she did not look out the window on Friday she could see the large removal van, but no people.

'They are in, dogs as well.' She told the girls when they called with their news.

'Dogs?'

'Yes noisy, barking their heads off all day'

'Really Auntie, how nasty.'

'Do you think you could walk that far if we took you to meet your new neighbours?'

'Of course I can, but I don't want to go. If they want to see me, bring them here.'

'Okay we will go and get them.' Outside they were rolling up with laughter they did not have any dogs or cats that crapped.

'Woof, woof' went Grace.

'Stop it, come on let's go and cheer her up'

'Where are they then?' she asked as they came back alone.

'Here Auntie'

'Nobody here only you two'

'That is it Auntie, it is us two, we have moved next door to you' said Jean.

'And our two dogs' whispered Grace

'Shut up will you.' Auntie was amazed.

'You never said'

'No it's a surprise' they gave her a cuddle and made her a cup of tea.

'Hope you got that price down it was never worth the money they wanted.'

'Down a bit' but they had paid full asking price as so many people were looking to buy these houses. As she drank her tea, Auntie said

'I didn't know you had two dogs.'

Many years had passed since then, Auntie did say one day what well behaved dogs they had. Grace told her they had died. Auntie was most upset and sorry to hear that, it was nice to hear the guard dogs next door.

'Silly old fool, was all your family like her?'

'Yes just like me.'

'I didn't say that.'

'No but I must be to put up with you at times.'

'You don't put up with me, you love me.'

'Unfortunately I do.'

Jeremy Horden-More, Grace's ex-husband felt he put up with much, married to Grace for so long, there had been plenty he disliked about her and very little he liked. Her hair that was not bad and he liked her name, Grace.

What he did not like was the way she was bringing up their daughter. As he thought it distracting and not suitable, he sent the child away to boarding school. Grace hated it but she had no say in the matter. The child did not care at all. Jeremy named their child Flavia, wonderful, thought Grace what a name and never called her anything but Flay, much to Jeremy's disgust.

Not to cause his precious daughter any embarrassment, he never wanted to divorce her mother until Flavia had finished her education. She did not care at all and would probably have been less embarrassed than she was on open days at school when daddy could not get there.

Grace would arrive driving her sports car, far too fast, wearing jeans and high heeled thigh boots or in the summer very short mini-skirts. She was a popular mum with her school friends, they all wishing their frumpy mums, that look down on Grace, were more like her. However, it made Flavia cross as mums should not be as popular or dress this way.

She told her father and before she was sixteen they divorced. None of them misses each other. Birthday cards were the only event that they acknowledged, Grace sent her daughter a card with quite loving words and always her change of address when it changed, just so they could keep in touch if need be. Flavia sent her nice cards and it always had a pressed flower enclosed in it. A sweet gesture her mother thought sent to someone who you cannot stand.

'What a thing to say, bet she brags about you now you're not there.'

'If she knew the half she wouldn't would she?'

'Are you including me in that statement? My boys think we are great and they love you.'

'Oh yeah and so does your stupid husband'

'That is one thing I will agree with.'

Jean's sons on the other hand adored their mother and could see why she left their father, he was impossible and they were lucky she stayed as long as she did. They were first to leave home, getting away, not standing by her leaving her to cope with him alone.

Jean's parents died within months of each other, leaving their much inheritance to her.

'Leave him Mum you have money of your own now.' She did not leave it was easier to jog along. She kept her money away from him, and did not own up that she had so much.

Clive her husband, like Jeremy with Grace, his name was also the only thing she liked about him, but she certainly did not like his hair. Sometimes she looked at him and wondered where the person she married was? He went away and left this thing behind. Nothing resembled the man she married.

Jean would pull faces behind his back when he came to visit them as he often did.

'You've slept with him ducks, had passionate sex, unless your boys belong to someone else,' Grace would whisper to her making her pull more faces at the thought.

Grace when she left made sure Jeremy paid her a considerable amount of money, pleased to do so he allowed her more than she thought he would. A divorce soon followed and being a rich man she was bestowed a jolly good settlement.

When Jean and Grace met, they were two women not short of money, just short of love.

Jean was still living with Clive, but Grace was alone, not doing her admin at the town hall then but in some other boring job that she cannot remember.

She went along to one of Jean's dancing classes, just for something to do as she lived nearby, she often see people going into the hall. She paid a visit and met Jean.

From the moment, Jean held her to take her through a fancy waltz step they both felt something towards each other and progressed to being together constantly. They would go back to Grace's apartment after the class. When the dancing class folded because of lack of support, they met at Grace's home every evening instead.

Before long Jean left Clive, moved in with Grace then they both moved out of town into another apartment away from anyone they knew. Not that they cared, but there was Jean's school teaching work to consider.

She had never divorced Clive because of these reasons, people at school knew she had left him most having seen him did not blame her.

Her boys and their wives were pleased for her and they all liked Grace, she was great fun and made such a difference to their mother.

Neither of her boys had children, well not yet, and no animals.

'Why would we need animals when we have a hairy donkey for a father?'

The women settled for the evening on the sofa after their ham salad.

'What's on the box' asked Grace as Jean kicked off her shoes and relaxed with a sigh. It was raining hard, making a cosy atmosphere indoors. Jean liked to make an open fire in their Victorian fireplace it was not necessary with the central heating, but a nice feature.

There came a banging on the wall, Auntie.

'She's off again'

'Oh dear whatever is wrong now, dam well raining as well' said Jean.

'I'll go' said Grace as she leapt up grabbed Auntie's keys and in her bare feet ran next door in the rain.

'Got a problem Auntie' she called as she went inside.

'I can't shut the window and the rain is coming in over the sideboard' Grace could see the side of her bay window was wide open to the elements. She reached out, dragged the window back, and closed it, mopping up the puddles the rain caused.

'Why on earth did you have the window open wide like that?'

'It was only open a little but the wind caught it.'

'Of course it did, why open it at all?'

'To let the cat out' Grace tucking a rug around her chilly legs said she did not have a cat, and do not do it again.

'Would you like a hot drink?'

'No I'm fine, it was just the window, my programme is coming on now and you are stopping me from watching it,' she was dismissed.

Returning to Jean, she explained,

'Let the cat out?'

'Oh dear, it is some way gone time she is reliving' Grace threw herself back on the sofa, holding her wet feet high as wiping them on the coconut mat at the door for that purpose was uncomfortable in bare feet.

'I can see your knickers that he looked at, I thought they would be flesh colour, he has got an imagination, let me see,' she peered up Graces legs they are maroon and made a grab at the knickers to look properly.

'Hey careful they cost me eighteen quid'

'Good God, mine cost three pounds for a packet of five from the supermarket.'

'What those big cotton ones.'

'Yes the sort that Hugh Grant likes in the "diary" films'

'Here try mine on' said Grace as she quickly slid from her underwear. Pulling at Jean's large knickers she started to replace them with her own, smiling at Jean as she lay back letting her do it.

'This is turning me on' said Jean.

'I was hoping it might.'

Chapter Three

Auntie Agnes in her young days had done many things.

'In the fil-ums I was.'

'Yes dear you have told us many times, you were at the back in Alfred Hitchcock's Birds, doing a bit of screaming.

'No dear I was acting'

Another claim was she had been a suffragette in her youth, campaigning for her right to vote, this made them suspicious about her age. Put in prison once, never force-fed, as she would not give up her food for any cause. When she came out from her overnight stay in prison, which over the years had extended to a month, she was a bit subdued but never gave up the movement.

She made a big thing of voting with delight, and made sure that every female she knew did the same, even now with the effort involved for her to get there.

'I fought for this vote' she told the officers at the polling booths and they made a fuss of her.

She also helped to "ban the bomb" she camped at Aldermaston with all the other women for weeks. She had married three times, one he divorced her, is still living in France the other two dead. She had no children, no dogs or cats, never had cause too.

'The only animals I ever had were those three husband of mine' she would remark.

A surprise came to their door, a great surprise. Jean answered the ring on the doorbell Grace was busy defrosting the freezer.

'Yes dear, can I help you' she asked of the young girl who stood there holding a huge grip bag.

'Does Grace Horden-Moore live here?' Flavia asked seeming that the women with the long skirt, flat shoes and baggy jumper would not be Grace.

Quick to realise whom the visitor was, as Grace called herself plain Grace More. None other than her daughter would know her full double-barreled name.

'Yes, yes' looking her up and down Jean

answered her question.

'Do you wish to come in?'

'That was the idea' she said. Gosh just like her mother, this was going to be difficult Jean could tell.

'Well 'em, just a minute please, I had better fetch her' Jean closed the door sharply as the girl had a foot raised to enter.

'Grace' she called

'What love?' all arse and legs she mumbled from the bottom of the chest freezer.

'You have a visitor'

'Me, oh bring him in then.' Wondering what him she thought it could be Jean said

'It is a Her'

'Just the same.'

'You bring her in.' Jean said to her.

'For Christ sake can't you see I am busy?' She chucked the ice slice back into the freezer grabbed a towel to dry her hands and stomped to the front door still wiping. Leaving Jean grimacing as she listened.

Not yelling, as she expected but she came back quietly, followed by her daughter Flavia.

'Sorry Mummy but needs must.'

'I would never recognize you how grown up

you are and so beautiful.'

'I know'

'Crikey' said Jean softly 'and modest' as she filled the kettle with fresh water.

'Give me that bag, take a seat' Grace said, not taking her eyes off the young woman.

'Come to stay have you?' enquired Jean.

'For a bit, well perhaps just a couple of nights.' Grace was still staring at her grown child with disbelief.

'I can't see any resemblance to who you were when I left, or see your father or me in you.' She said looking closely at the girl.

'Do you think she looks like me Jean?'

'Not a bit, talks like you though.'

'Does she?'

Talk they did for the next hour, if it was not for the freezer to be refilled they would still be at it come teatime.

Unwrapping the frozen food from the sheets of newspaper Grace, replaced everything back into the freezer in order. Jean continued making their tea.

Flavia just sat there.

They had tea together and talked some more. It appeared that father, Jeremy had a new girlfriend, many since Grace left actually, but the latest one was from her old school.

'If you don't mind, that means the same age as me. A cocky bit, all over father in front of me, I just had to leave.'

'Did he care?'

'He doesn't know.'

'Oh that's trouble love, best you phone him after tea in case he is worried.'

'Worried not a chance, I might phone him though tell him to up my allowance considerably as I will have more expenses.'

Sounds like she is going to pay her way thought Jean, working her way would be more helpful, perhaps she will wash up these dishes.

'I will air the spare bed and find new sheets' said Jean.

'That's okay Je, I'll do it, you wash up' Grace waved at her, then they disappeared upstairs with Flavia dragging the large bag behind her. Jean obeyed the waving hand.

This looked like it was going to be fun.

She was still in bed when they went to work the next morning, leaving their spare front door key on the hall table in case she wanted to go out, and a note by the kettle that she could not miss telling her the key was there.

When Jean got home after school, earlier than Grace as usual, the key was still there, so was the note. Surely, she was not still in bed. Jean opened her bedroom door slowly, sure enough, she was still there. Is this what young people did, stay in bed all day?

Jean carried on as usual, preparing their tea, wondering what her tastes were. So far, she had just picked at food, some stupid diet she suspected. No way was she making anything special it would be the same as theirs, like it or not.

When the potatoes were boiling, Jean could hear movement in the bathroom. Grace coming home looked around for her daughter.

'Not gone has she?'

'No such luck, she's just got up and gone into the bathroom'

'Oh tired then.' Grace had a brief wash at the sink, as she could not get into the bathroom, just hands and face, then she started to lay the table.

'Not on our laps tonight?' observed Jean.

'No let's sit here' Flavia came into the kitchen yawning, but clean and dressed.

'Your showers not very warm'

'Sor-ry!' said Jean waiting for another moan as she put a plate of food in front of the child.

'Oo yummy'

'Done something right' Jean mumbled.

After they had eaten their meal, Grace asked Flavia would she like to meet Auntie Agnes.

'Where is she?'

'Next door'

'I've got an Auntie Agnes who lives next door, that sounds good.'

'No dear it is Jean's Auntie, not yours but we all share her.'

'Great, lead on.'

They were not sure if Auntie Agnes grasped who she was though they did explain thoroughly.

'You never told me you had a daughter' she said to Jean 'but then you never told me you had two dogs'

'I haven't seen them yet, two dogs?' a surprised Flavia looked at Jean.

'No they died, very sad it was too, the white one was a lovely thing, clever knew every word I said' Agnes filled Flavia in with her lies.

Jean sighed. As they left Auntie said,

'Bring that young girl again I liked her, who

did you say she was? It is a long time since I last see her, don't make it so long next time.'

Returning back next door, Flavia remarked 'She's as old as Moses'

'It does appear so.' They proceeded to tell her Auntie's adventures. She was impressed, 'Ban the bomb, they were hero's, were you there,' she asked Jean.

'No dear nothing heroic about me apart from keeping my husband alive'

'That's pretty good, how did you do that?' She imagined Jean saving him from drowning or waiting for the helicopter to rescue him off the cliff top with a broken leg.

'Kept him fed and watered when he wouldn't work'

'Oh I see' a disappointed Flavia nodded.

The next day was much the same. When Jean got home from school, Flavia was watching television in the sitting room, but she was not dressed.

'Hello' she called cheerfully.

'Not up long then?' said Jean looking at her.

'Yes I have actually but I didn't know how to put the boiler on for hot water so have not showered yet.'

'Didn't you have cold showers at your boarding I thought they all did?'

'No way, you must be joking, we were all girls. It was not Gordenstoun, that place where they sent poor Prince Charles, I think they did it on purpose to have a go at him. Bet all the others had hot showers. You can't possibly get clean in cold water.' She mumbled away to herself.

'I read from that you consider us not clean as our water isn't very hot?'

'No I didn't mean you'

'Yes well, our hot water comes from a storage tank and I think you will find that we take most of the hot water in the morning. As the house is empty all day the boiler is not set to come on again because there is no need for it to heat up until the afternoon when we return.' Explained Jean, wondering why on earth she was making excuses for no hot water to this young woman.

'I am not picking fault, sorry if it sounded that way.'

'I will override the control then it should be hot in no time,' said Jean.

'Ta, shall I make you a cup of tea?'

'That would be nice thank you.' While

drinking their tea Flavia asked

'Do you two sleep together?'

'It does appear so your mum is always there when I wake up.'

'I thought so.'

'Is it a problem?'

'Not at all, I am not an innocent only child, I went to boarding school don't forget, you cannot miss much there.'

As soon as the water was hot enough for her, she disappeared into the bathroom and was still there when Grace came home. Relating the conversation about their sleeping arrangements as that was all she could say about Grace's questions what had her daughter been doing today. Jean asked her,

'Has she telephoned her father?'

'How do I know? I'll ask her.'

During tea, on their laps this time, Grace asked her about the phone call to her father.

'Yes I phoned he didn't seem to notice I wasn't there'

'Does he mind where you are?'

'I said I was staying with friends and I needed more allowance as the rent was high'

'Perhaps we should charge her rent' Jean

said later.

'Jean, she is my daughter do you mind.'

'Should you not tell him the truth?'
'It is the truth you are my friends.'

Eventually finding out how much Flavia's father allotted her for an allowance Grace was shocked.

'She gets more than my take home pay one thing I have always said about Jeremy was he could be generous. I suppose that is easy if you are wealthy.'

'Perhaps you should have stayed with him then you wouldn't have to do admin.'

'I don't think I had a choice in the matter, I didn't leave, I was told to go.'

'I forgot, it was me who left to be with you wasn't it'

'Certainly was not before time, wait until Flay meets Clive.'

'She already has, he called in for ten minutes yesterday, and I introduced them.'

'Oh what did she think?'

'She didn't think she said'

'Oh cripes, what did she say?'

'She said to him you smell.'

'Ho, ho, dear me.' Grace laughed like Father Christmas at the thought, what did he say?'

'He said he did not, she followed with yes you do mate you stink.'

'And?'

'He walked out.'

'My, sorry about that Je.'

'No don't be, it is true isn't it, suppose you do have to laugh at her.'

'All this confidence she has got. Allowance or not she needs a job. I'll see what I can do at the Hall.'

'How you getting on with old Brady now you are in the cupboard?'

'Just the same but don't see so much of him. I keep my door open all the time in case I get claustrophobic, when he walks past he always looks in the door so I open my legs at him.'

'Grace!'

'It is better than I thought it would be many people pop in for a chat with the door open. They bring me in cups of coffee and stay a while.

'Doesn't he say something?'

'No he is frightened of my open thighs.'

Next day Grace asked him were there any jobs for Flay.

'Oh Mr Brady' she called as he passed keeping her legs shut and put on a sweet smile. He nearly fell over, coming back he said,

'Yes!' from the door, he did not come in. She explained about her daughter, threw in university but knew Flay did not get that far, she could always apologies for being wrong when they found out.

He said she could work there, share her office, share her desk sitting opposite her legs was a good idea and share her salary.

'Bastard' she said loud enough for him to hear as he carried on his way.

Going through the normal channels Flay did get a job there, admin in another office in another part of the building. Keeping her own name, no one knew she and Grace were related.

Talking to Flavia one day, Jean asked her did she do similar admin to her mother?

'Mum doesn't do admin.'

'She always says she does.'

'No she is more important than that. Something to do with accounts, wages I think, it is Mrs Moore this and Mrs Moore that, she has a lot to say.'

'I never knew what about old Brady?'

'Oh yes, he is important too, Mum can't stand him, I don't know why.'

One time when snuggled and quiet together Jean said

'I found out something'

'What bit of gossip have you found out then you nosey little devil, tell me?'

'You don't do admin.'

'Oh that, did you think I would climb those bloody steps every day for an admin salary?'

'Grace lazy or what, I will not love you if you get fat.'

'Yes you will there will be more to love.

Chapter Four

While washing up together Grace asked Jean,

'Why don't you take Flay to the six o'clock class?'

'Do you think she would like it?'

'Don't know but it would save me going.'

The next lesson Jean did just that, but it proved to be a disaster.

On the way she asked if Flavia could dance, she certainly could, every dance you could think of, they taught her at boarding school and she was not bad at it either.

She helped, that was nice, showed interest in the learning, chatted to the dancers. They liked her they were talking about everything except dancing.

She took their entrance money at the desk while Jean got her music set up. Suddenly announcing loudly to everyone,

'As I explained to each of you at the desk the rent has gone up and next week it will be three pounds and then following on it will be five pounds. Sorry about that but it is still cheap, can't get much for a fiver can you, defiantly not for an hour.' They all nodded in return. Jean had to look away, grinning at the prospects, they would not pay more she was sure of that.

Flavia partnered each of them in turn helping them understand what Jean was teaching.

During a waltz, while Jean was on the stage looking for her samba music, Tracy came up to her,

'Your daughter is a dirty cow' shocked Jean spun round

'I beg your pardon?'

'Look at her.'

There was Flavia dancing with Tommy Albright, very slowly not really dancing more just rocking from side to side. He had his right hand on her ample breast, moving it in time with the music. She was leaning her lower body towards him, feeling his erection on her stomach, watching him closely with interest, as everyone else in the room was. His eyes were closed he was in a state of ecstasy.

Jean pulled the plug on the music it came to a sudden halt. Tommy came too, not realising where he was at first, then wiping the dribble from his mouth he rushed off to the, one and only toilet that they shared.

'That's great' said Tracy 'gone in our toilet to finish off what she started.'

Completely flustered Jean was not sure what to say. Flavia joined them,

'Bet he hasn't had a grope for years'

'Bet he's never had one' said Tracy. Composing herself Jean could see this had caused a disruption, everyone had been watching, no way were any of them in a mood to learn more.

'It is nearly time to finish I suggest we call it a day'

'Aw' they all said, having enjoyed the floorshow.

'Will someone bang on the toilet door and tell Tommy we are going. Hearing this he soon came out, head down and rushed off.

'Good was it?' Grace asked Flavia.

'Yes great fun, nice people.'

'I could think of some words to describe that

lot, nice people would not be my first choice. Did she give you a fiver for helping?'

'No, but she can keep it, can't pay for enjoyment can you' and she ran upstairs.

'What?' asked Grace as she looked at Jean?

'Tommy Albright that's what.'

'Oh no, we should have warned her.'

'No need we should have warned him.' Jean continued, explaining the episode, by the time she had finished Grace was in hysterics.

'God I wish I'd been there, I wonder if it will put him off or he will be more eager, could turn him into a good pupil.'

'Good at what one wonders.'

Then she told her about the little announcement and the price increase.

'She never, I wonder how they will take it?'

'No one will turn up next week, you see, she can pay the hall rent.'

Jean was wrong they did turn up and three new people. Tommy was there all wide-eyed and innocent looking for Flavia, who Jean had refused to take.

Grace was at the desk, everyone produced a fiver. She said nothing just took the money as if it was normal. Later she crept over to Jean.

'Hey thirteen at a fiver each, that is sixty-five quid.'

'Really I don't believe it, did they moan?'

'Not a word' Jean was not sure if the new people had heard about the floorshow or had really come for lessons, time would tell.

The lessons stayed at five pounds and the numbers increased by another two. Jean offered to pay Flavia part of it but she refused saying not to worry as father had increased her allowance she had more than enough.

Flavia started to make friends at work, which Grace thought was good, they were generally a nice crowd. Young people all about her age, both sexes. Flavia felt she needed a car but managed by cadging lifts from her friends. Parking really was a problem in their road, fortunately, they could spread on to Auntie's space.

'Good job I don't still drive my jeep' Auntie told them, another lie, who knows?

'Your bus would have been a huge problem' Grace laughed at her.

'Don't be silly I have never had a bus, don't think I could manage one of them.'

'Haven't you? That's a shame.'

'Stop winding her up.' Jean told her off.

They were all sitting in the kitchen, not doing much when they heard Ron calling Jean from his garden.

'What's up love' Jean called back from the open window.

'Can I come in?'

'Yes sure.' He lifted his long legs over the fence and came in the back door.

'Hello' they all said to him, he had met Flavia before. Looking very crest fallen he sat down.

'What's up mate' said Grace looking at him worried and wondering why he needed them. 'Is it her again?'

'Afraid so I just had to get out don't want your house devalued because a murderer lived next door do you.'

'Oh my, is it that bad?' Flavia looked at him in astonishment.

'At times I could do her in and have no regrets, I really could.' Flavia moved back a little still listening intently but not liking what he was saying much.

'What's her problem Ron?'

'It is you two, now three.'

'What, don't you bring us into it, especially my daughter, she is young, not a women of the world yet.'

'I would disagree there' said Jean. Flavia put her tongue out at her without Grace seeing.

'Who says it is us, you or Angela?'

'Angela, not me, she recons I fancy one of you if not all of you and I don't.'

'Thanks, what's wrong with us, most men fancy us, especially my boss and her husband and her Tommy. Flavia was trying to smother a giggle.

'I didn't mean like that, oh dear I shouldn't have come in here.'

'Ron here drink this' said Jean as she handed him her cup of tea she had just made.

'I was going to say tell us from the beginning but I don't think that is such a good idea now.'

'Yes tell us it sounds interesting' asked Grace wanting to know all the details.

'It went on for ages, all morning she hasn't stopped, for days actually and I just said, yes you are right and I am going in to see them all, all of them right now, then I called out to you. Oh flipping heck.'

'Where is she now?'

'Don't know but she was watching me climb over the fence.'

'Oops she will be knocking on the door in a minute with a meat cleaver in her hand.'

'Tell you what I'll go round and see her'

'No Grace that is not a good idea either, you know what you are like.'

'What am I like for heaven's sake?'

'Ask Mr Brady'

'You go Jean' Ron suggested.

'No I don't want to, if any one goes it must be you back home in a little while. Drink your tea, its calming.'

'I'll go' said Flavia

'Certainly not' her mother replied.

'Help, who is that?' Flavia cried out as they heard loud banging on the front door, not the bell ringing.

'Blimey it's her with the meat cleaver' said Grace making out to be shaking. She went to the door, before anyone else moved, they all listened.

'Hi Ange'

'Angela please'

'Your name is a bit like and angel in fact

without an A on the end you would be one, are
you an angel?'

'Oh do shut up you silly bitch.'

'Ere, ere don't you get nasty with me.'

'Is he here?'

'Who love?'

'Jesus, give me strength!' said Angela

'No he's not here, only us, try the church'

'Ronald' she yelled up the hallway.

'Oh him, he's here.' Those in the kitchen
were listening with mirth, until she said he was
here then Ron said,

'Oops here it comes'

'Let me in' Angela said as she pushed past
Grace calling

'Ronald, Ronald' he did not say a word.

'Come in Angela do' said Jean as she
crashed the kitchen door back with some force
'would you like a cuppa as well?'

'No thanks' Ron didn't look at her or speak.
Grace came in put her arm around Jean and
muzzled into her neck, trying to send vibes
back to Angela that the last thing they would
want would be her husband.

She didn't take on the hint she was so cross
with him and proceeded to have a one sided
argument about one woman not being good

enough for him and thought he could have the choice of the three next door.

He still did not look at her. Flavia thought the whole thing great fun laughing at her.

'And that one there,' she said pouncing on Flavia 'is nothing but a child.'

'I'm nearly twenty, well over the age of consent' she said indignantly.

'Are you dear, I didn't know you were that old,' said her mother.

'Old? Mummy, she'd love to be my age,' she said pointing to Angela who she hardly knew.

'I meant that old as in I have a twenty year old daughter, are you sure about that?'

'You are all crackers in this house, why on earth you should fancy any of them Ronald is beyond me.'

Ron stood up suddenly and noisily giving the table a knock, as Jean grabbed hold of it to steady the cups that rattled.

'Well I do so there' he shouted at his wife pointing a shaking finger at her, 'any one of these ladies is better than you and if they would have me I would move in tomorrow.'

'Here none of that' said Jean. Grace stepped in to confront him.

'Ron the only way to tell you is straight out,

you are barking up the wrong tree dear, we are not looking for a man, we have each other.' She gave Jeans neck a good muzzle and kissed her on the lips.

Angela took a sharp intake of breath,

'Your lesbians, I knew there was something strange about you lot, why you are after my husband I don't know. Come on Ronald' she got hold of him by the shirtsleeve and with his mouth open, he let her direct him out of the house. Flavia was clapping with delight,

'Wow, wow, wow, go on Ange take your little treasure home' she called after them as she ran to the front door to slam it shut.

Jean and Grace laughed, but both said it was not good to fall out with ones neighbours like that but it was fun.

'She will spread the news up and down the road to be sure.'

'We will deny it. But we will tell the truth how her husband fancies us any of us do you mind and my daughter who is not twenty yet.'

'I say you do have fun you two. It would almost be worth changing to a lezzie, but I would miss cocks too much.' With that, she grabbed an apple from the fruit dish and moved off into the sitting room.

'What did you say? What did she say?' Grace not believing her ears asked Jean.

'I wasn't listening.'

You had visitors' Auntie Agnes told them.

'Don't miss much do you, how did you know that, bet you know who it was as well?'

'I was putting the cat out and saw them two from the other side leaving your place in a hurry, dragging him out she was.'

'Oh you did, did you, and the cat again eh?'

'I can't stand her stuck up mare, he's alright but she should not live in this town, it's not posh enough for her.'

'She should live in the Cotswolds'

'That is right, I knew someone who used to live there, her husband still does I believe.'

'Give me strength' said Grace.

The next day was Saturday, house cleaning day.

'I thought I'd go and have a chat with Auntie' said Flavia.

'You, why? To get out of helping us with the housework?' asked her mother.

'No, well yes, if I can, but I just thought I would have a chat with her before she gets into her television.'

'Okay clear off, you are no good here anyway' they passed the morning doing their jobs. Flavia was ages with Auntie Agnes. Eventually returning when she was hoping the cleaning would be over.

'Guess what?'

'No I am not guessing, you tell me.'

'I have seen the cat.'

'Auntie's cat?'

'Has she got one?' asked Jean

'She really has got a cat, I don't believe it.'

'Yes it was sitting on her lap as bold as brass. Just came in and took up residence she said. I have just been to the corner shop and got her some cat food, all she gives him is fish from her freezer, not that he minds.'

'I bet he's a ginger tom, they always roam.'

'Yes you're right, ginger with white feet, beautiful creature.'

'He must belong to someone.'

'Auntie said he was starving and uncared for when he first came in through her window and now he stays there with her all the time.'

'Thank goodness, I was beginning to think she was going batty' said Jean.

Later Jean answered a gently ring on the front door to find Angela and Ronald on their front doorstep, holding hands and a bunch of flowers.

'We wish to apologies' Angela said as she thrust the flowers at Jean.

'We are sorry and do not wish to fall out with or neighbours, which can prove to be very difficult' said Ron.

'We feel the same do come in' Taking them into the kitchen again Grace was surprised, Jean give her a "watch it" looks running her fingers across her mouth meaning zip it up.

'Look how nice, flowers.'

'I was just saying how upset we both were it is not nice to argue with next door neighbours, no matter what the problem is' said Ron.

'Yes agreed Angela'

'Shall we just forget it then?'

'Would you like a cup of coffee or something?'

'No thank you all the same we have just come back from the shops and have to unpack our shopping another time perhaps afraid not just now.'

'Anytime' and Jean see them out again.

'You were on your best behavior, surpassed

yourself for that.'

'Bloody nearly wet meself, there was me thinking I could introduce her to Jeremy and get rid of her to the Cotswolds.'

'Good idea but Ron would be a pain, unless Flay would take him on.'

'He is old enough to be her dad.'

'So, her dad has one her age.'

'Yes but her dad has got money that makes a man very attractive. Ron's got sod all.'

Did you hear what Flay said about cocks, my daughter must have been around.'

'If you had seen her with Tommy you would have no doubt about that. He will remember her all his life.' Flavia came downstairs.

'Have you been talking about me?' she received no answer, 'I heard Tommy's name mentioned, and who was that at the door, and who sent you these flowers?'

'For God's sake,' said Grace as she turned the radio on, and Jean put the flower in water.

'I'm going out'

'Okay love, see you later' called Grace to her daughter as the door slammed.

'Peace, what's this? Who is that? Life is not your own.'

'Come ducks shall we open a bottle and chill out in the sitting room for a while?'

'Good idea' Grace turned the radio off.

56

Chapter Five

In between outburst, their life was calm and happy.

Jean had just finished her class at school, music and movement involving her piano playing, not great, but she could manage a thumping for the children to, supposedly do their dance steps.

The young children run madly around letting off steam and winding themselves up into a frenzy, making it difficult to get them settled down to a desk lesson afterwards.

Making this turmoil the last lesson of the day was her idea. No matter how gracefully she made the dancing instructions they went crackers, in the large hall running, jumping, boys bashing each other. Samantha Brown liked to pull her PE knickers up into her arse crack and showed her bottom to everyone as she danced causing the girls to laugh and the boys to grab a pinch at her backside.

Some would hold hands others would not. Peter would never join in always sat watching because he had something wrong with him, his leg or his arm, usually his foot.

'Can't dance if you have a bad foot can you Miss?' One or two gave her hope as they tried and enjoyed the music.   At times, she did wonder if she was any good as a dance teacher at all, what with the six o'clock class.

Worn out with shouting above her piano thumping, trying to keep an eye on any roughness ready to bring a stop to it. Then to get them to sing which was always screaming instead of singing, she had to sing along with them.

Her class was on the way home now, telling their mothers what a lovely time they had. Mums were pleased they liked it but often could not see the point of this mayhem.

Jean collecting her music together, securing the piano, she could see Miss Collingwood their head mistress making her way towards her.

Miss Collingwood was walking with the aid of two sticks now, so as not to give her the length of the hall to manage Jean went towards her.

'Hello dear, all the babies gone? I just came for a quick word as I wanted you to be first to know, I have given in my resignation and I will be leaving at the end of this term.'

'I am pleased and sorry as you know' said Jean 'pleased you will get the rest you need and sorry to be without you.'

'Not to fret, shit happens.'

'Oh I have never heard you say a rude word before.'

'Yes well never seen me on sticks before have you? Never told you I quit before. Do come into my office and have a coffee before you go home. Marion will be there.'

'That would be nice, nearly ready here, I just have the classroom to pack up, see you in a bit'

During this coffee meeting, they discussed Jean's advancement to being Head Mistress.

'I will only be a phone call away if you have a problem, so never feel you have to deal with anything alone.' Jean though sad at losing her friend was excited at the prospects for next term, which would be another school year.

Telling Grace they celebrated, they went out for a meal together.

'Not celebrating too quick are we?' asked Jean as Grace ordered more wine.

'This is just a warm up, wait till you get the job' Auntie and Flavia, even Clive was pleased for her, this would round up her career, teaching all her life, she would most likely not take a class again, certainly not thump musical movement on that old piano.

Miss Collingwood wore her cap and gown, in school, only the cap on serious days, the beginning and end of term assemblies, however, always floated around in her gown. No mistaking who she was, just a little frightening for the first year children.

Jean would not do that, but no need to wear old clothes that often got paint dabbed on them or splashed with child's vomit as has happened many a time.

She would wear a suit, yes always a suit that gives an "I'm in charge" look, she gave a giggle to herself, and that I am "In charge".

The formalities were just beginning, interviews with the powers-that-be, and the board of governors, oops she did not look forward to that one, and the education board of something.

Three interviews she had to attend, they had all her references and recommendations but still asked many questions. Repeating herself over and over. At last, it was 'over'. She just had to wait.

'Celebration' said Grace.

'Nothing to celebrate yet'

'Interviews over that's what' so they went for another meal and more wine.

Bumping into Conway Knight who was one of the school governors, he was very kind and polite, pleased to meet Grace who just said 'likewise' incase she put her foot in it.

They had a titter when he left, hoping that blonde bit he was with was his daughter, but very much doubted it.

Term ended, all their farewells said to Miss Collingwood, the whole school sang to her "Wish me luck as you wave me goodbye." She cried. It did sound sweet all these young voices singing the old Gracie Field's number. Jean and all the staff went into their summer break.

She cared for the two girls while they worked therefore they had nothing to do when they got home, a little rest for them.

She also cared for Auntie and Buster, as they had named him, as he busted the window.

The problem with the window was leaving it open for him it had busted, broken, and a man called in to repair it.

'A cat broke this, get away, how big is it?' he wanted to know.

'I could fix a cat flap in your back door would that help?' He suggested to Auntie.

'What a good idea, yes do it.' He soon fixed a lovely flap. Buster would have none of it and sat by the window meowing.

'Waste of money, that was' claimed Auntie.

'Leave it to me' said Flavia, 'come Mummy I need you.' Armed with Buster and a plate of food they set about showing him back and forth through the flap, he spitting and fighting.

'Don't let him run off Mum, grab him.' Grace did grab him, not too gently and he shot back in again.

'There he did it'

'Not willingly, he is scared of you he'd have run through a train tunnel to get away.'

'Get away from me?'

'Gently Mummy talk to him nicely' they tried again, still not liking it and getting fed up, he wanted the food, so he climbed in the flap knocking the screen up and off, frightened himself and Flavia as he knocked the food over the floor and ran upstairs.

'Bloody thing' said Grace as she opened the back door and returned indoors.

'Where the devil is the teacher? She should be here doing this' they made a cup of tea for Auntie and themselves.

'Did he do it?'

'No' said Grace as she reached for the biscuits.

'Keep still, look' Buster was sniffing then tapping the cat flap, pushed his head out and as quick as a flash went through it, running up the garden, hard to say with fear or delight.

Later listen Auntie was banging on the wall.

'Bet it's that cat come let's go and see' there he was sitting on the windowsill to come in.

'Told you' said Auntie, looking pleased that she was right.

'Let me think' said Grace, pull that curtain across so he cannot see in and I will rattle the cat flap. Placing a plate of food a little way from it, she rattled the flap and sat down watching as she kept the rattling up.

Soon a paw appeared, dabbing and pushing the flap, this went on for ages, then just a nose pushed in sniffing the food, a bit further and his head appeared, very slowly lifting one foot at a time pausing, but not for long he soon came back to devour his food.

Flavia and Auntie were watching from the door, they cheered and clapped frightening the life out of Buster and he ran upstairs.

'I never thought he would do it, well done' said Auntie.

'That Jean should be doing this not us as she's the teacher, where is she?'

Unbeknown to them Jean was summons to her last meeting and told the headship news.

Not all was well she did not have the job.

A new person would take over and of all things a man.

'But we are a female staff'

'Yes that is not advisable today and one of the reasons we could not give the post to you.'

'One of the reasons, what other reason?'

'At this point Mrs Bradshaw we would usually say nothing personal but I am afraid it is, we did have to take into account your home circumstances, 'er if you understand what I am referring to.' He shuffled papers looking a little embarrassed.

'I certainly do and can see now that the

headship was not what I wanted after all, good day.' She left with her eyes stinging with tears.

Sitting in her car, it developed into a weep.

'Bastards' she told the car still extremely upset. It took a good ten minutes to compose before she could start to make the journey home.

'Here you are, no tea ready yet' said Grace as she sat at the table shelling peas, 'we've been doing a bit of teaching, we needed you, but we managed, dam good at it we are as well. Buster now uses his cat flap.'

'I wish I could say the same' Jean related her news, with disbelief Grace and Flavia listened.

Grace burst into tears,

'Come love it's not that bad.'

'It is I wanted to say my partner is the Head Mistress.'

'You would not say that even if I was Prime Minister, you are not a lesbian remember.'

They held each other as Flavia quietly slipped from the room leaving them together.

That evening Jean and Grace sitting alone, no television, reading books.

'I know shall we have a party to cheer ourselves up' said Grace putting her boring book down. Silence followed, Jean was not listening, was not reading either, just looking at pages.

'Did you hear me?'

'Yes dear I'm here aren't I?'

'What did I say then?'

'Er it is a good book and something about it is cheering you up.' Jean guessed.

'I'll say it again'

'If you must.' Grace turned to face Jean, who was getting herself braced to listen.

'We are going to have a party'

'You never said, you never asked if I'd like one.'

'I did, what do you think?'

'Not much, who would we have to put up with?' Jean had a very disinterested manner.

'A party Jean, give me strength, you don't put up with people at a party you are pleased they came.' She got up and found some writing paper in the sideboard.

'Give us your pen' she said to Jean. She handed over her very expensive, beautiful to write with, that she uses constantly, pen, with trepidation, fully aware that Grace could be very clumsy. She started to make a list in two seconds it was getting long.

'Who have you wrote down?' Jean was looking dubious over at this long looking list.

'Auntie'

'Auntie Agnes, you must be joking'

'We would have to ask her or she would moan or fall out the window being nosy trying to see our visitors.'

'Who else?'

'Your two boys, their wives and Clive. May Hunter from work and her latest fella. Anyone from the teaching fraternity? That is up to you. And her and him from next door.'

'What Angela and Ron, not exactly a rave up, more a punch up if those two come.'

'A few of Flay's mates, the crowd she mixes with at work would liven anything up. I think she has a boyfriend by the way, tell you about that in a minute. Let's see anyone else.' Grace took a breath gazed at the list, licked the pen preparing to add more and went 'errh looking at the pen in disgust.

'Clive, oh can you imagine?'

'You don't have to own up to him being yours, you felt sorry for him sleeping in the shop doorway or something, so gave him an invite, okay?'

'Her and him, do you think they would

come even if they did get an invite?'

'Yeah, being neighbourly couldn't resist it.'

'How many is that?'

'Let me see, counting and adding us over a dozen, then there is your mob and Flay's mob.'

'I haven't got a mob and I don't expect Flay has either.'

'Oh yes she has I have seen her with them quite a little group of "know all's" they are, yuppies I suppose they like to think.'

'From work you mean, my goodness don't you mind Mrs 'I am in charge' More?' Ignoring her Grace continued

'Think who you want to ask'

'Nobody'

'I like the spirit you are putting into this.'

'You said to cheer me up, bringing reminders from Victoria School would not cheer me up at all, I'd sooner bring Tommy Albright' she slammed her book shut and dropped it on the floor.

'Now you're talking, free entertainment, he would dress up and do a strip for a quid.'

'I'm going to make a cup of tea, want one?'

'No make mine a vodka and juice I am in a party mood.'

Jean did give in and invited two of her colleges from school, one a teacher and her husband and another who dealt with the naughty children with so much patience and a heart of gold, she was everyone's friend, not married so came alone.

Next door, both sides loved the idea.

'Couldn't stay at home with a noisy party next door, could we?' said a delighted Angela.

'She could go out' said Flavia 'bet she causes a rumpus. I will dance with Ron just to get her going.'

'No you will not we have seen your type of dancing, we don't want him dribbling on our carpet.' Auntie said she would come but could not stop long because of Buster and her television programme.

Flay had her own list, that grew daily.

'I think we may have to put a limit to your guests dear, this house is quite small and only one toilet' her mother told her.

'I was thinking about that' said Jean 'one toilet is really no good, where could we have another one built?'

'Nowhere right now, not before our party.' They set a date and bought no end of readymade frozen snacks, from the local supermarket. They also did a party service, plates of cold meat and Chinese bits to pick at, along with buying more than adequate booze. Flay and Jean sorting through the collection for suitable music,

'Not the samba love.' It did cheer them up, apart from keeping them busy preparing for days, they were pleased to welcome their friends, when asked what it was in aid of they just said to cheer us up, it was agreed by everyone they all needed cheering up. Therefore, it was a success.

Auntie stayed longer than anticipated, moaned when Jean took her home that she had missed some programme.

'How about I buy you a recorder then you will not miss anything?' suggested Jean.

'One of them things, no thanks it is not that I go to many parties and miss things is it.' Jean got her settled in her chair, turned the television up loader so she could not hear her noisy neighbors next door.

Buster was on Auntie's lap as soon as she sat down and Jean could see her eyes closing, she would be asleep in no time. How many whiskeys had Grace given her, she crept out.

Flavia and her friends took over the dancing in the very small place left to dance.

'Come on Jean show us how to do it you are the expert' some gave her a shove, she grabbed Grace and they danced together, very well. Grace was a good dancer too, they all watched, impressed as they pull back giving them more room.

'Can you do line dancing?' asked Bobby one of Jeans sons.

'Yes, can you?'

'We can, find some suitable music' Jean found "Rock a Billy Rock". Bobby jumped up with Pam his wife, they all lined up following the experts in front with the steps until they turned round and they fell over each other. Laughing they all agreed to try again.

Angela kept popping home to use her own toilet, taking one or two ladies with her as they were queuing up to use the only toilet in the girl's house.

'Auntie Agnes has two toilets you know' Jean told Angela.

'Where has she put them?'

'She still has the original outside Victorian toilet as well as the one upstairs in her bathroom, came in very useful when she was gardening she always tells us.'

'Not keen on an outside one myself, some people along this road have made a downstairs loo near the front door, if you walk along you can see small new windows, or a porch.'

'I have never noticed'

'I will show you.'

That is how Angela and Jean came to be seen slowly walking arm in arm along the road one Sunday afternoon observing possible places to put a second toilet.

Ron had his fair share of wine, dancing all the time made him thirsty, not having to drive home another benefit. All the drivers refused alcohol. Ron was beginning to go over the top, he danced with Grace and Jean in turn Angela did not mind. He found the dance with Flavia most stimulating, as Jean watched closely. At times rubbing bottoms together then noses, no other touching Jean was pleased to observe.

There was a young man Flavia preferred as a dancing partner, tall with fair hair, they knew each other well you could tell.

Clive had not moved all night, he had the same can in his hand that he had started with. Jean topped up his plate of food often, which he did eat heartily.

The evening was ending. Angela dragged Ronald home, holding each other up. Bobby took Clive back.

'Didn't enjoy himself much did he Mum'

'Has he 'er ever enjoyed anything?'

'Not that I can remember'

'Thanks for asking us Mum it was nice' said her daughter-in-law.

Reviewing the happenings the next day all three of them relived the party with many 'did you sees?' and 'what about?' They agreed it was a good party but would have been better if they had two toilets.

Chapter Six

Jean went next door to find out if Auntie had enjoyed herself after her longer than anticipated stay.

'Coo ee' she called loudly as she could hear her television blaring out. Still sitting in front of her television she had slept there all night, but taking a closer look she could see Auntie was not asleep, she had died.

Sitting in her chair, comfortable, the look of no struggle or pain, passed away in her sleep. Jean knocked on the wall several times. Following that rather quickly, answering the knocking Grace and Flavia came to the door.

Jean greeted them with such a sad face they guessed what had happened.

'Whew just sitting there' said Grace 'do you think it was all too much for her?'

'Does appear so'

'Too much whisky do you think?'

'No I only gave her one glass'

'And me' said Grace.

'And me' said Flavia.

'Well so she had three glasses of whisky'

'Four' said Flavia 'she asked me for a top up, it was a large one she kept saying "more don't stop" so it was a big glass full.'

'Maybe that was the problem'

'Oh God, I killed her' Flavia started to cry.

'Stop that now, we have to telephone for someone, who? The police ambulance or doctor?'

'I will phone her doctor he will know what to do.' After an emergency call, Jean eventually spoke to their doctor.

'Don't touch anything' was his instructions and he was there quickly with the ambulance and police. After enquiring who found her and when, they were asked to leave while they removed Auntie's body.

The following week was hectic. Jean took some time off to deal with no end of little but time consuming, problems. Surprisingly Auntie had made a will, apart from four charities everything she left to Jean. Not much money but the house went to her. Judging by the amount she had left to these charities, Jean would sell her house to pay the charities, but she did not want it anyway.

One thing they did get that they actually did not want was Buster. They had to give him a home, locking the cat flap to stop him getting into the empty house caused him so much confusion he sat by it most days wanting to get back in, then he would try the window.

Calling back the man who fitted the flap he soon removed it altogether and put one in the girls back door, within no time Buster used that and enjoyed their company, having a choice of laps to sit on.

Auntie's funeral was over and her house was cleared, but not in a hurry.

A strange thing happened at her funeral, there were not many people there but there was a man sitting away from the family, softly crying.

'Excuse me' Jean said to him, 'we are only going back to our house for a cup of tea, would you like to come with us?' Thanking her kindly with a foreign accent, he declined.

'Wonder who he was?' said Grace when they got home.

'Foreign he was'

'What sort of foreign?'

'Hard to tell as he was very foreign'

'What do you mean by that?'

'Well not American or Australian'

'That cuts it down then.'

'No I mean English was not his native tongue spoken with an accent as Americans do, he was foreign, difficult to understand.'

'Wonder what his connection with our Auntie was?'

'We will never know, some long lost admirer'

'Perhaps he was a suffragette' said Flavia.

'No silly, they were all women'

'Ban the bomber then'

'I think they were all women too.' They forgot all about him until a note came through their letterbox the next day.

'It's from the foreigner, he's French.'

'How can you tell from a piece of paper?'

'French words there look sil vous plait, oh and he has changed his mind and would like to visit us this afternoon at two o'clock.'

'Wow can I be here?' asked Flavia.

'Yes you must.' At two o'clock, they were ready and waiting to greet their guest. It was nearly two thirty and nothing.

'Not very punctual is he?'

'He's foreign maybe he is on French time?'

'They are in front of us, so he would be early.'

'Just wait and see.'

'That's all my day waiting, ten more minutes and then I'm off.' Grace said this as a taxi arrived and out got the man in question with another man.

'Here look two of them' Jean welcomed them both and invited them into the sitting room. Flavia soon appeared with a tray of tea, after adding another cup and a bigger teapot.

After the introductions, they were Pierre Roos and Andre Roos. In his broken English, he got straight to the point.

'Agnes Roos, your Auntie was my mother this is Andre my son, her grandson.' He stopped, looking at them. They were flabbergasted, even Grace, who spilt some tea in her lap.

'I am sorry Mr 'er Roos, I don't understand my auntie had no children, perhaps you would care to explain yourself?' This opened the floodgates. In broken, hard to understand English corrected by his son and helped when he could not find a suitable word, he told his story. They listened intently, dumfounded.

Auntie had married his father and lived in France with him for many years they had a son Pierre, this was he, late in her life, auntie was into her forties. When Pierre was twenty, his father died. Agnes left France and her child.

'I could come with her to England but preferred to stay in France. I was cross she left and did not like her for it, so did not talk.'

'She told us she had an ex-husband in France, but she did not at all, it was a son.'

'Yes and a grandson, which she knew nothing about.' He said pointing to Andre.

'How did you trace her, how did you know she died?'

'A what, what?' he said looking at his son for help.

'A solicitor, her solicitor the one who made her will' said his son.

'Oui' said Pierre.

'I am having trouble taking all this in' said Jean.

'You two are cousins' Grace told her.

'No my auntie was married to his father.'

'That's right your mother and his mother were sisters, therefore you are cousins.

'Yes Jean mums right.'

'And you two as well?' Andre said the Grace and Flavia.

'No we are no relation only Jean.'

'My father was right, he said only Jean, and his English is not so good. We have to return to France tomorrow so we came to explain and invite you for a he meal at our hotel, yes, no?'

'Thank you very much, I think it must be yes, if you are returning so soon.'

They had a nice evening together and a good laugh when they got home. Pierre produced some old photos they could just about tell it was auntie, she resembled nothing of the auntie they knew. Jean could see her mother's likeness as she remembered her when young. He showed her one photograph that Jean particularly liked and he told her to keep it. She asked if they would like to see Auntie's house and maybe take back a memento, they declined. Parting sadly, relations that Jean could tell she would never see again.

Auntie had always told lies and right up to the end, she had been deceitful about Pierre. There was her story somewhere that they would never know.

'Usually people tell the truth before they die you'd have thought she would have said she had a son.'

'Are but she didn't know she was about to pop off, it is not as if she was ill and confessed on her death bed.'

'No crafty old thing, in the end all she cared about was old Buster here.'

'Yes her tale of France we will never know, we can only guess, but I'm not going to start down that road.'

They had her house to sort out, not a job they relished.

'Shall we have one big mad clear out, or a bit at a time?'

'A bit at a time, no rush is there?'

'Suppose not.' It took several months in fact six months before anyone would say it was near empty. The called an estate agent to price it, two prices, as is, or modernized.

That was another thing to consider another time, no rush.

Jean's son Bobby who was married to Pam, had no children yet, they lived within walking distance of his mother, a good walk mind, but close considering how far some families lived from each other. They actually lived nearer his father, Clive. Pam liked Clive, why ever she should, baffled everyone.

'Make him wash more' Grace told her.

'I can't do that'

'Suggest it then'

'No he would not like me to be personal.'

She could see the resemblance to her husband, this laid back attitude, he did not care much about anything, and very patient. He had this hangdog appearance waiting patiently for you, just as some dogs do. Surely, she did not want to see Bobby get like his father.

Jeans other son Paul was the same. They were jollier than their father, they did enjoy life, which could not be said of Clive. He never laughed or looked happy or showed any interest in anything. This miserable person was uncomfortable to be with, apart from his disheveled appearance, if he were spotlessly clean, it would make no difference to his personality.

Jean often thought back to what he was like when they first met. He was jolly then, she was sure, easy to be with nice company he worked in a garden centre that is where they met. He was very knowledgeable his aim was to have his own garden nursery one day. He had an allotment, the nearest he ever got to his own nursery.

They married and lived in a flat, no garden so the allotment was an asset, they both attended it, Jean like the open air but not the digging and more often just sunbathed while Clive worked.

It was nice, she had her babies then short of cash as they always were, she looked for a way to earn more money deciding to do some teachers training. Before long she had a teaching post in a local school, her boys were in a baby's nursery they were soon to start school.

Life was getting better, they moved, with a small deposit they bought a house with a small garden. Clive was happy he made the garden appear bigger with his ideas, still keeping his allotment.

Then the beginning of disaster his garden centre went into liquidation. They pulled it down dug over the gardens and houses built in its place.

There was no offer from a new buyer or an offer of employment for him. No other work became available not the sort he was looking for, he worked for a short while in a DIY store, it drove him up the wall, he left.

Plodding about on his own in the garden or the allotment all day, he became withdrawn. He started to show no interest in his sons or Jean. You could not say he was unpleasant as he said and did nothing, but he was annoying, especially to Jean.

At one time, she thought he was suicidal and was concerned. She spoke to their doctor who could see what she meant and prescribed some medication that seemed to make him worse. He never worked again.

The allotment was uncared for, all the hours he spent there, he mainly spent in his shed he had a comfortable armchair in the shed looking across the plots many other plot holders came and had a chat with him.

Jean could see his life, get up, do nothing, go to bed, what sort of life was that. It was not the medication making him dopey as he soon forgot to take it, as if it was making any difference anyway.

He was not worried he never worried about anything, just accepted whatever was thrown at him.

Choice words from Jean she always threw at him, one-sided arguments about his life style achieving nothing.

It was about this time as he totally ignored her she decided it was his hearing, so she took him for hearing test and eyes while she was at it. Nothing was wrong at all.

She gave up in despair.

For a man that did nothing he made a terrible mess. Just walking into a room, he made it untidy, because he looked a mess, he made the room look untidy, but when he left, it still looked the same. What did he do?

Jean's answer to this was to put locks on several doors in his own home, in that way Jean had less to do when she came home from work. The kitchen was awful. Their two boys left home at a young age, who could blame them, they moved in with friends, sharing.

Before long, Jean met her lifesaver Grace.

She spent all her time with Grace and it was not a difficult decision to move in with her permanently. At first, she did not think Clive understood, even now she wonders. By his rarely spoken words, anyone could tell he expected her to return to him one day.

He never showed concern or worry that his

wife lived with a woman and what that implied, he just waited around doing his dirty old but faithful dog bit, sad really.

'I am going away for the weekend' Flavia told them at breakfast.

'That's nice dear going far?' asked her mother with little interest just being polite.

'Well....going to see dad actually.'

'I see, you should it has been a long while now. Will you tell him you are staying with me?'

'I wasn't going to, shall I?'

'No, no if you think there is no need.' Grace said glancing at Jean who had her head down in a nothing to do with me manner.

'How are you getting there?'

'I am going with a friend, he is driving.'

'Oh I see' said Grace again but much slower. Jean got up and started to clear the table, preparing to wash the dishes not looking at Grace but feeling her anxiousness. There was a long pause as Flavia finished drinking her tea.

'Lucas, you remember Mum, at the party, tall, blonde and chukka'

'Chukka?' questioned Jean, never hearing that expression before, but guessing what it meant. Ignoring her Flavia continued.

'Lucas has a brother who lives near there we are staying with him for one night. Then we will call in and see Mr Hogan-Moore before returning.' Clearing the last of the dishes from the table and handing them over to Jean, Flavia called the conversation to an end with a hurried remark,

'I can't hang around here talking to you old bids, I have to wash my hair.'

'Old bids, do you mind?' as she went out the door Jean added,

'Chukka must mean he is, jolly nice.'

'Jolly bloody lovely!' Flavia called back as she ran upstairs.

'Well what you make of that' she said to Grace.

'What an arse upwards way to talk, why couldn't she have just said Lucas is going to see his brother, I am going with him and will see dad while I am that way.'

'Putting words into her mouth are you?'

'Not at all it just made me uneasy for a moment, going away, seeing her dad, friend driving, must be me, I found it strange. Still all appears fine, and this 'er Lucas is a nice bit of stuff what I remember of him.'

'Yes, a good dancer, I had a boogie with him' Jean grinned 'does he work at the town hall as well?'

'Yes all her friends who came to the party work at the Hall.' Grace casually, shrugging her indifference.

'So you knew them all'

'Well, only sort of, they are nothing to do with me.'

'Beneath you by the sounds of it after all you are Mrs Moore in the cupboard.'

'No matter what, he is very nice this Lucas Westwood' Grace pondered.

'You do know him then? You already knew his surname, or have you made enquiries?'

'Yes I know his name so what?' Making it obvious she was not going any further with that conversation, they dropped the subject with Jean smirking and Grace trying to look uninterested in this Lucas person.

Equally, they had a nice weekend, after the usual Saturday morning bustle, they made a trip to Brighton. Sunday was a nice day early on Grace suggested they went out it was going to be hot later.

'Yes nice, somewhere high to catch the breeze, let me think where shall we go?'

'How about the coast?'

'Yes better still, Brighton, I'll drive'

'Won't take us long then?' Knowing the speed that Grace drives. She has a 'nippy' car so she nips in and out between the traffic taking risky chances with Jean gasping every five minutes.

'That is what I was thinking if you drive it will take all day.' Jean was a steady careful driver, never one to rush, the opposite to Grace, who would rush to catch a cold.

'Shall we set a time limit to get there by?'

'No! Take our time and enjoy the journey.'

'I will just take a flask of coffee for the journey, no food, plenty in Brighton to choose from.' They were ready and there remarkably quick, the longest time they spent doing anything was trying to find a parking place. It did appear that everyone had the same idea and had flocked to Brighton for the sea breeze.

They strolled along looking for somewhere nice to eat. Not feeling at all out of place, they held hands, a thing they did not do often. In Brighton there could be seen many couples of the same sex openly together.

It was a nice break for them and they were pleased to have made the effort.

Coming home late, they found a strange car outside their house. Flavia was already home.

'Hello darling did you have a nice weekend?'

'Where have you two been?' seeing their sun blushed faces, ignoring her mother's question.

'Brighton, it was lovely, do you know whose car that is outside our house?'

'Yes it is mine'

'Yours, didn't know you could drive?'

'Oh yes one of those things dad made me do as soon as I was old enough, then he did not have to drive me about anymore' she told them 'And the car?'

'It's mine it was stuck in his garage. I asked him to get it roadworthy as I needed it you know battery and whatever things go flat if cars are not used regular. There was me thinking it is a long while since it was driven, but apparently not, one of his floozies has been using it, no harm done, but still a cheek, bet she is missing it already, he will have to buy her one now.'

'Where is Chukka' asked Grace.

'Gone home Mum, some of us have to work tomorrow.'

'Don't we all, I'm heading off to bed now, beat you to the bathroom' said Jean. There was a rush to get there first Jean won.

When alone Jean commented to Grace that Flavia didn't say much. Grace had to admit, she did not, why, nothing to say or covering up.

'Then you didn't ask much did you?'

'I will, or she will tell us perhaps.' Now she has a car she will be out all over the place, we will not see much of her I suppose,' her mother pondered the future.

'I don't think she will be all over the place I think she will always be in the same place.' Jean was right Flavia spent most of her time with Lucas, at his place. He had his own apartment along with a friend lodger whose rent helped with the mortgage.

There was no need for them to spend time with Grace and Jean. Their lifestyle changed, it was quiet, no banging on the wall, they never thought they would miss that, and no Flavia rushing around. Jean got bored, never being a television fan, Grace came home one day to find her in her unused study, the place where she needed to mark her schoolbooks that the first years never had. She was sitting in front of her computer.   Salad for their tea was prepared and in the fridge.

'Hello love what are you up to?' asked Grace as she took her coat and shoes off.

'I am writing a book.'

'Wow, I said you could. Is it to be about Aunties life?'

'No it is about Monorails.'

'Do what? Those railway things that hang in the air, suspended instead of running on rails, what do you know about them?'

'Quite a bit actually, there are no simply explained books about them so I thought I would write one.'

'God how boring!' Grace left her to it.

After they had eaten their salad Jean asked can I read you a bit that I have wrote so far see what it sounds like to you?'

'No you dam well can't I am not interested in monorails at all, go away with your silly book.' Jean huffed of into her study.

An hour later she returned, coming into the sitting room she joined Grace.

'I have changed my mind'

'Should think so too'

'I am going to write about Auntie after all. I am going to go through all those papers of hers that we have got, to get names and dates, try and put her lies into order.'

'That sounds better ducks, can I give you a hand it will be fun.' Grace gave her a nudge.

'Yes of course if you fancy it, research!'

The next evening they started, it was a job, everything was so muddled, all her husbands and the different names mentioned. They found some birth and death certificates, they were helpful, at least they don't lie.

'Oh I wish I had asked her more questions when she was alive.'

'She would not have told you or probably forgot, then made something up. Look at this handsome fellow in this photograph it just says George B on the back, who is he?'

'Perhaps we will find George A in a minute.'

'I think the reason she told lies was that she had forgotten so much, she did not want to appear stupid so just made it up. We were gullible enough to believe her most of the time so she carried on. If we presume the lies were the truth it will make a good story.'

Jean made notes, most evenings scratching through Auntie's papers.   No attempt at writing the story yet, Grace began to think she never would.

The whole idea faded off rather quickly as she was asked to give dancing lessons at the local Conservative Club, Monday evenings between seven thirty and ten o'clock. Sequence dancing, one week and Line dancing the next.
'This is going to be different to the six o'clock class. These people really want to learn,' she told Grace.

Jean was excited about her new class she had to do a lot of preparation, brushing up on her steps it was a long while since she had taught sequence dancing, but at onetime it was her favourite lesson, elegant and slow. Nearly all retired the people in her class were good dancers.
The line dancers were a jolly crowd, the music was jolly but the steps could be difficult to remember, they did a lot of counting and going wrong but that was all the fun of it.
Sequence dances they would repeat all the time they enjoyed them and wanted to do

them repeatedly. However, line dancers were different they had to learn something new every lesson. There was always something new coming along. The best she could, Jean wrote the steps down for them, printing sheets off so each pupil could take a copy home and practice.

She would dress up for this class, a flared skirt, or jeans a cowboy hat and scarf and in addition, the boots of course.

Grace not to miss any of this she joined in, she could only do a little but was prepared to learn. They danced and practiced in the conservatory and on the patio, most evenings. Jean had a good collection of music, but still wanted more, buying anything, she considered necessary.

She started with the sequence dancing Grace did not have a clue but went along just the same.

The entertainments manager at the Conservative Club telephoned to inform her they had thirty-six names put down for her class and come the day there would most likely be more.

'Thirty six, I have never had such a large class' she told Grace. They had inspected the dance hall that they were to use, it was excellent, tables and chairs around the edge, but still plenty of room to dance on their well sprung floor.

On the appointed evening once Grace had set up her music getting there early, people started arriving.

'I have counted forty four so far' said Grace. Couples gathered ordering their drinks, then settling at a table many coming over and saying hello to them.

'Friendly lot' said Jean.

Shortly starting her programme with an easy dance, she could see tuition was not going to be necessary all of them were experts.

She spoke to the manager during a dance, saying she did not think they needed teaching they were all very good. Not to worry he told her, just organize them and help if you can see it is needed. She felt a fraud as a teacher, but this was just what they wanted a whole evening spent just sequence dancing, not just one now and then.

Thanking them both at the end of the evening and confirming they would be there next week for the line dancing.

Line dancing proved to be a different kettle of fish. No expert in any dance, Jean really had to teach simple dances, it took a while to get any perfection, but the going wrong was all the fun of it. If one went wrong often another would follow and before long you had a whole line or more all wrong.

'No, no, no' it would cause laughter and they would start again.

For some unknown reason, there never were as many men at these classes.

'Too difficult' Grace told her 'don't want to be made a fool of when they go wrong.' Yet it had started as a man's dance, all that stamping and thumping, kicking should suit them.

Flavia kept out of their way most of the time, she was always in a rush to get out and get away from them as they one, two, and three, stamp, and kick, turned all the time.

Everything went on hold, no book-writing auntie's house stayed the same. Flavia often called out to them asking had they fed Buster as he wrapped himself round her legs.

'Oh no, could you dear.'

Flavia and Lucas not only working together spent all other time together and yet it still was not enough for them. She could not move in with him as there wasn't room with his lodger there and Lucas considered it not fair to ask him to go, they would wait till he moved out, but he didn't and had no intention.

An idea came to them both, almost at the same time, they needed a bigger place.

Flavia burst into work one morning finding Lucas straight away before starting work

'Auntie's house' she almost shouted at him. Taking a little while to register what she was talking about then a huge grin came on his face,

'Of course'

'You wouldn't mind living next door to my mum?'

'Never, she is great, it would be excellent' they discussed the possibility at length after work and could see no problems Flavia would approach Jean and Grace.

'I will come home with you.'

As they went in the front door, they could hear the music.

'Stamp, stamp, two stamps there, left foot now turn'

'Oh it is like this all the time?' said Flavia to Lucas.

'Coo-ee' she called, they could not hear. Slowly going into the conservatory, where they were practicing they made them jump.

'Hello there is a surprise' they both gave Lucas a brief kiss in welcome.

'We haven't seen you for ages Chuck how are you?' With a frown at the name Lucas reported he was fine.'

'I am thinking lets open a bottle' said Grace.

Once settled with drinks in hand Lucas said

'Go on then to Flavia.'

'Mm' the women looked at her in anticipation.

'We want to buy auntie's house'

'What' they were both amazed, 'no you can't do, next door to your mother.'

'Yes we want that' said Lucas.

'Oo er I would never have wanted to live next door to my mum.'

'You are, sorry if I am being rude, not the usual type of mum, are you' said Lucas.

'This is a turn up, have you given it much thought?'

'Oh yes' they said not telling her they only had the idea that day.

'Well if your serious I have to say the inevitable, can you afford it?'

'I have my apartment to sell' Lucas explained.

'And dad will provide the rest' said Flavia.

'You can't be sure of that'

'I can, if not I will say I am moving back and bringing Lucas with me, he will give me a blank cheque on the spot.'

'Christ I wish I had a dad like that I did one thing right when I married him.'

'Mum!'

They all took gulps of the wine as Jean topped up the glasses.

'No price has been arranged with that estate agent yet. As is, or modernized?'

'Oh as it' Lucas informed them they wanted to do the changes their way.

'Right a phone call tomorrow.'

'Can I just ask, no wedding?'

'No wedding Mum, maybe a baby.'

'Or a dog' added Lucas

'Or both?' suggested Jean.

'Then a wedding' said Lucas.

'You haven't asked me to marry you' said Flavia.

'No I haven't but I might, I think.' She punched his arm.

'Don't torment her Chuck we know if you

do marry her now it will only be to get your hands on her half of the house.'

'Tell you one thing we would like, can we have a look next door?'

'Certainly I will get the keys for you.'

Once inside auntie's house alone, which incidentally Lucas loved, they planned and added, taking out this or that, he asked Flavia,

'Why does Jean keep calling me Chuck?'

'Oh my, there is a story she must forget you are Lucas it will pass.' However, it did not Jean never used any other name for him except Chuck, nobody ever explained the reason to him and he got use to the name and never enquired again.

Flavia did ask her father for financial help and unexpectedly he wanted to see the house. He could by all means she apprehensively said. The estate agent came up with a price that was acceptable to all, only father now to approve.

Mr Hogan-More stuck to his guns and insisted on seeing the house. Flavia told Grace.

'Fair enough he is paying for it. You must arrange a suitable day with him. Crikey Jeremy coming this close, it is years since I clapped eyes on him.'

'You don't have to see him dear' said Jean.

'Oh but she will, hiding behind the curtains trying to get a nosey at him' Flavia looked at Grace 'won't you Mum?'

'Yes if I can, will he bring his bimbo with him I wonder?' Before he arrived, they informed the estate agent of the circumstances. At no time was he to mention the owner lived next door, he alone was to deal with it completely.

Pleased to be told as he did find it a bit confusing, but now understanding this client's father would be paying and the position she was in, made all clear.

A rather large, and very expensive car arrived in their road, he could not park outside the house as the car was so long. Jeremy got out of his car and viewed the parking spaces with disapproval, before looking at the house.

'My God he's bald' an amazed Grace uttered to Jean who was also hiding behind the curtains. Flavia and Lucas were with him, 'no bimbo such a shame.'

Grace got a good look at her ex-husband as

he walked back from the only place into which the car would fit. Apart from no hair, he looked well and prosperous as always. He approached the front door, which was right next to theirs, as they are in most rows of Victorian houses. They dodged back from the window, not that he would have a clue who they were, just nosey neighbours.

'Would you have recognised him?' asked Jean.

'Oh yes apart from losing his hair he is exactly the same, stuck up bugger.'

'I wonder if he would know you.'

'Of course he would I am no different than the day he married me. Bet I could get into my wedding dress with ease, if I hadn't ripped it up.'

'You didn't'

'Yes in front of him too, chucked the shredded dress at him in the bedroom telling him he should have married a parlor maid or waitress, can't remember which now, someone in a pinafore, he didn't want a wife.

There it stayed for weeks in bits all over the bedroom floor, cost him five thousand pounds that dress did, I kicked it every time I passed the mess. I wouldn't let my daily help tidy it up. She thought I was mad.'

'She was shrewd,' said Jean.

The visit took ages, was this genuine interest or just for Flavia sake trying to make it look good.

'He is in the garden' called Jean 'poking about at the top end.'

'I say mind he doesn't get his designer shoes mucky.' Grace called back, not wanting to him to see her she kept away from the kitchen window.

'Tall and slim' called Jean

'Yes and bald, ha ha.'

'You are being catty?'

'I hope so'

They left smiling it looked like all went well.

'Do you think he will visit his daughter often?' asked Jean.

'Shouldn't think he would visit at all, he will treat it like another boarding school with Lucas in charge.'

'It is good of him to put up the cash though.'

'That is only pocket money for him he will not miss it.'

'Just thinking if they do get married you two will have to meet'

'Mmm I know, that happens at all weddings when the parents are divorced another added unpleasant thing for all on the day. Cross that bridge when we come to it.' Grace relaxed in an armchair with her own thoughts about Jeremy tumbling around in her head.

Flavia and Lucas were ecstatic.

'Guess what, he is paying for it all.'

'Does that mean his name on the deeds?'

'No mine, as we are not married he suggests Lucas keeps his place until times when we are a couple legally then all can go into one pot. We can live where we like for now.'

'A better arrangement I suppose a business head you see.'

'I can rent my place, get an income from it, pay the mortgage and some over' said Lucas.

'We won't need to bring the lodger with us he can stay where he is and there is room for at least two more people sharing.'

'Good old dad' said Jean 'I have to give quite a bit to auntie's charities they will be pleased.'

'Who are they?'

'Four of them, all strange, all in the need of money, one is the local cats protection society, they will be very grateful. Another is the local, all of them local, gardening club they are to have a coach trip out to a garden somewhere, their choice and all their club fees paid for a year. In addition, the same for the wine club, not a coach trip, but their fees paid for them, a free year like.

She also wants eight trees planted, all different I forget which at Topbarn Common and a wooden bench placed under one with her name on a plaque and 'Rest here awhile'. The solicitor will deal with it all and I am to have what is over.'

'Well done auntie and thank you'

'Let's have a bottle to go with that come along, Chuck help me choose.' Jean and Lucas went off to rummage down her wine store. Grace and Flavia had a happy hug.

The purchase of next door went ahead.

Father never came again or showed any interest after that visit, he paid whatever price they agreed. The estate agent did a lot of bowing and scraping to the man in the limo. Whoever he was and what relationship to who made no difference to him, he was the man with the money.

Lucas wanted them to do the updating improvements themselves, Flavia agreed. It became a hobby taking all their spare time.

'Get fed up with that they will' said Jean.

'I think it is my turn to cough up some of her grandparent's money to go towards these improvements and call in the professionals.' However, they would have none of it.

'We want to do it ourselves, that way the house will become ours.'

That is what they did, taking no end of time, not rushing. Flavia stayed with Grace and Jean and more often than not, so did Lucas. The first room they worked on was their bedroom, enabling them to sleep there. It was nice to wake up in the morning to a completed room. They moved all their clothes into the wardrobes and then decided they did not have enough cupboards, so made more alterations. They had long dumped the kitchen along with part of the bathroom into the back garden.

Using her mother's facilities Flavia enjoyed the mainly weekend working. This went on for over a year, not at all perturbed they continued slowly but Grace had to admit it was looking beautiful.

Come the summer they left the house and Lucas started on the garden, Flavia sunbathed.

They acquired a helpmate Lucas needed it he really had not got a clue what to do in the garden, apart from cutting back and making things look tidy in general.

Surprising them all Clive helped Lucas they had all forgotten how knowledgeable Clive was. Jean had not forgotten, there was not much he did not know about gardening, but could Clive remember?

He could, and remembered well, he was proving a great help to them.

They had a large garden, Jean could see him looking over the fence at their garden, and eyeing him suspiciously, she asked Grace, her opinion if when he had finished there he offered to attend to their garden.

'Yes let him, he looks happy, I didn't know he knew how to do happy.'

Chapter Seven

The new dancing classes were going well, the numbers swelled more came for line dancing than sequence, line-dancing nights the hall was full to capacity with dancers.

Jean still held the six o'clock class, blundering along with the same indifference. They had heard about the line-dancing success,

'Can we do line-dancing?' asked Tracy.

'Yeah' all the others in the class called out.

'I don't think so dear, it is not as easy as the dances you do here'

'Easy? I don't think this is easy'

'I've seen them do it, it's all stamping and kicking you just follows the one in front.' Jean could see she was not going to get out of this easily she started to think of a very easy dance.

'Okay, line up and follow my steps' she turned her back to them and slowly she called out counting all the time.

'Turn, repeat and again, one, two, kick

stamp, kick stamp, stop.' Silence, she turned round to look at them all. They had all finished together in time, all facing the same way, all smiling.

'Did you get it?' she asked

'Yes can we do it again?'

'One more time then we will try with music,' they did it one more time, Jean kept glancing behind at them, not believing they were all together.

'Music now is everyone ready?'

'They were excellent' she told Grace 'I can't believe it even Tommy and George, I could not say who was best because they were all good.'

'Are they coming to the Con Club?'

'Oh no, not that good, but I think we will do a lot more line dancing, forget the rest especially the samba, it is too hard for them.'

'I'm coming to see this' said Grace impressed with what Jean was saying.

'That's the first time I have known you to volunteer without me begging.'

'Come of it, I always help you'

'Under duress, you do.'

The next six o'clock class they were both there early, wearing cowboy boots and hats.

'I've got boots look' said George the first to arrive.

'Smashing boots' said Grace 'seen mine?' she lifted her skirt to show off her boots as well

'I will need a hat' George said

'Here take mine' and Grace plonked her hat, a bit small for him, on top of his head. They all came in with a rush.

'Can my sister join?' asked Tracy

'Sure' said Grace as she looked over at Jean.

'This is Karen' said another. Rushing to start someone called for "Cotton Eyed Joe" and off they went.

'A new dance now, are you all ready to pay attention to new steps?' They all shuffled in line and waited for Jean.

'This one starts with stamp, stamp' they all started practicing their stamps.

'Stop, stop' called Jean 'all together now after three. One two three, stamp stamp' and away they went following Jean, when they turned they followed Grace at their rear.

'Two more practice runs, then to music' it was a success.

'I like this club can I join?' asked Karen.

'Club' Grace mouthed to Jean.

When they were home, Grace suggested to

Jean they should call it a club, which sounded better than lessons or class.

'Okay I go along with that, what club?'

'The Six o'clock Club, it has to be.'

'Right that's it.'

The next week they all came dressed for the part. The girls had flared skirt or jeans and the boy's jeans check shirts and waistcoats. All of them found a cowboy hat from somewhere.

Another week Jean took some photos of them, putting one in the window facing the street. This resulted in more members for their club and now they had two lines of dancers, soon to be three.

Flavia said she would come, Jean told her to keep away from Tommy.

'I will bring Lucas that will put him off.'

'Don't be silly dear, Chuck would hate it.' However, he went just the same and enjoyed it following Jean's every word.

Next, to invade them was Bobby and Pam, the experts. Bobby taking over one dance, showing them something more difficult, and to Jean's surprise they managed to do it. She was pleased to stand back and watch her pupils.

As she watched them she was getting ideas

for her babies at school, they could stamp, clap turn round and certainly kick. She would work out a dance suitable for them.

Miss Collingwood had long retired and Mr Digby taken over. Passing through the hall during one of her classes, he asked her what the children were doing. She invited him to watch. Jean worried if he would approve, but he was impressed. As he was watching the young children following dance steps, not just running round in "rings" as they liked to call their dance circles, he could see an achievement.

Jean played slowly on the piano for them but could not do both, play the music and show them steps.

'Come here let me play' said Mr Digby and he took over the simply tune Jean was playing as they followed her steps. For babies they were so good, stamped and jumped in all the right places. Mr Digby praised them all and gave them a round of applause.

They giggled, but looked pleased.

Clive paid Jean a visit when he had finished gardening for the day. He had a rolled up large parcel under his arm.'

'What's that?' she asked looking at it suspiciously, as he held it out towards her.

'It is a rug for Buster.'

'Oh do cats like rugs, I thought cushions were more in their line, rugs for dogs.'

'He will like this rug' he put it on the chair and left, declaring

'I have worked hard today, I'm off home.'

'Have a bath, eh Clive'

'A bath?'

'Yes dear it will help with the aches and pains you will get tomorrow.' He left not liking the idea much but he would have a bath. Jean got the fresh air spray out and gave a good burst around.

'What's that' asked Grace when she got in from work seeing the untouched parcel.

'It is a present for Buster from Clive.'

'Oh' unimpressed it stayed where it was until after tea.

'You going to look at this present or is it going to stick here all night?' asked Grace as she pocked the parcel.

'Open it then' called Jean from the sink as she washed up their tea plates.

There it was a rug, a large filthy rug.

'Where's that been?' asked Flavia.

'God only knows, Clive produced it.'

'Say no more.' They rolled it up again and put it in the utility room, forgetting all about it.

When Lucas called that evening Flavia told him, he just had to have a look.

'I see what you mean, but it could be silk and look under these stains are dragons, I think.' They all looked closely saying it smelt.

'Can I show my dad?'

'What for' asked Jean.

'He used to be an antique dealer, did I not tell you? He would maybe put some light to it.'

'The light of a match and have a bonfire' said Grace.

'Really, show him see what he makes of it, if you don't mind contaminating your car.'

'I suggest you get it cleaned' Lucas's father told her on the telephone the next evening after his observation, 'it would probably cost about two hundred pounds to get it cleaned professionally but I would guess that it could be worth about five hundred pounds. Where did you get it?'

Flabbergasted Jean had to tell him it was not hers and relayed the present for the cat.

'What do you think?' he asked.

'I think I was about to throw it out, but yes by what you say let us get it cleaned, where do I take it.'

'I will take it to a specialist in London if I may'

'By all means, thank you.'

Two weeks at least went by and Jean had another phone call, this time from the rug cleaner in London informing her it had cleaned up perfectly and looked very nice.

'I have a customer who is interested in buying it if you would like to sell, he will pay sixteen hundred pounds for it, maybe more.'

'My goodness, I don't believe it, no I don't want to sell it, but I do want to see it.'

Jean told everyone, Lucas was very pleased for her and they all told Clive. He said it was for Buster and did not want it back.

'Good job too he would muck it up again in no time,' said Grace. Lucas brought the rug back, neat and securely wrapped they stood round for the unveiling, like a butterfly it emerged from the chrysalis wrapping.

'It has dragons, oh it is beautiful'

'Are you pleased with it?' Lucas asked.

Jean who had not said a word so far was smiling with pleasure at the rug.

'So very much Chuck it is the nicest present my husband has ever given me.' They laughed at her and took the rug into the sitting room.

'Not in front of the fireplace in case I have an accident when I clean out the grate. Just here in the middle.' Jean indicated with her foot the centre of the room. Lucas and Flavia placed it straight. It did look good.

'You're not concerned that people will walk on it?'

'No point in having it hidden away, I want to see it.'

'What about Buster?'

'It is his.'

'I don't think he will harm it, he will like it.'

Buster did not like it, he would not put a foot on it. He walked round it, sniffed it, sat next to it but never touched it.

'Perhaps it is the dragons, they put him off.'

Not long after the appearance of the dragon rug Buster had to take tablets.

'That cat has got worms' declared Jean.

'What makes you so sure of that?'

'He eats like a horse and is still hungry, and I have seen him at the end of Flavia's garden watching for the field mice that Clive is disturbing with all that digging he is doing, mice can give cats worms.'

Jean paid the vet a visit and came back with tablets and instructions how she was to administer them. Buster was collected held on the table while all three women tried to get these tablets down him.

'First the vet said put some in his food and with any luck they will be gone.' Grace put one rolled in some cat food in his dish.

'Not one dear, four.'

'Four? All at once?'

'Yes, then another four in two weeks.' Hidden in the cat food went four tablets.

'There's a good boy, he has taken one, and another.'

'Oops, he spat it out' said Flavia as one plopped on the floor.

'Where are the other three' asked Jean.

'One still in the food look, and another on the floor, oh you just trod on it.'

'Grab him Grace.' Just managing to get hold of a grumpy cat Grace held him on the table.

'Right let me get some more tablets, the vet

said it was easy, hold him tight.' As she advanced towards Buster he kicked out and wriggled, 'hold him tight, really tight' yelled Jean, she tried to open his mouth 'just push the tablets to the back of his throat, the vet said.' He spat, and hissed at them, she quickly moved the pill towards the open mouth, he bit her fingers, scratched her arm, and lashed out at Flavia. She let go of him.

'Look what he's done' as blood gathered on her arm from the scratches.

'It's only blood, hold him'

'No Way!' Grace let go as well.

He ran off so quick they did not see the going of him.

'Honestly three grown women can't control a moggy'

'Tell you what, I will do the pill bit and you hold him if it is so easy' said Grace.

'Go and find him' Grace went off looking for the monster.

'Come and look at this' she called, they followed her. Looking into the sitting room, he was there. Sitting in the centre of the dragon rug staring at them with an evil face, if a cat could scowl he was doing it.

'He is sitting on my rug, oh!

That evening Grace and Jean sat in the veterinary waiting room, with a box.

'Ah Mrs Mason again, you were here this morning, worms, have you had problems administering the worm tablets?' looking at her badly scratch arm and giving a smile.

'Just a tad' said Grace sarcastically.

'Why is he making all that noise?' she asked of a cat in a cage howling as if it had his tail shut in a door.

'Oh him, he has had an injection and is under observation.'

'How can you stand it, put him somewhere else.' Grace said as she covered her ears.

'We did that last time and he collapsed so now I am watching him, as long as he is howling he is okay.'

'I think I would collapse if I had to listen to that noise all day.'

'He will stop soon, and then have a nice sleep. Anyway thank you ladies bring him in again in two weeks.'

'You have to give him tablets today'

'I did'

'Did you? Can you do it again so I can watch how to do it?' asked Grace.

'I certainly can't he has had his four'

'Four? What already?' While she had looked concerned at the 'howler', and Buster's attention was diverted by the noise, the vet had popped four tablets into the cat with no fuss. Jean had looked on in amazement, mouth open, pills in, mouth shut tight, throat rubbed just as he said why could she not do that?

Buster completed his course of medication and went back to not sitting on or touching the rug again.

Clive did like the rug when paying them a visit he liked to rub the surface.

'Wash your hands first Clive and don't walk on it.'

'I will take my shoes off'

'Do not bother I expect your shoes are cleaner than your socks.' The rug stayed impeccable for many years.

Chapter Eight

Jean's work with her babies was very rewarding, whenever she had a line dancing lesson with them Mr Digby, if he had the time to spare he would play the piano for her.

'I have given this some thought Jean they look so cute. Mayday we are having a May pole dance by the older children and several other groups of the older children will be performing, I will be inviting their parents to watch. Do you think your babies would perform or are they too young?'

'Yes I would like to think they could, they don't get nervous at this age you know.'

'Excellent, if it is not too much work for you I will put them on the programme'

'Can I dress them up, it would look so much better, instead of school uniform?'

'Dress up, how do you mean?'

'Cowboy hats, waistcoats and flared skirts with frills. My mothers are very helpful and if I put out a request they will soon come up trumps with suitable costumes.'

'Sounds very good, I will look forward to it. There is only about four weeks training for you, good luck with it.'

Jean was excited telling Grace they discussed the hats first, small hats, they came up with a few shops that may be able to help. Waistcoats check shirts, circular skirts they would wait and see what the mothers would provide.

Dress rehearsal followed much practicing, they looked so cute, hands on hips, while they danced. All had cowboy hats provided by Jean, some had boots, trainers were no good at all, as you could not hear the stamps. The children understood this and ordered which pair of their shoes was best.

A little makeup on the girls faces, bright red lipstick a must, ribbons in their hair, scarfs for the boys.

When they walked on stage and stood in line with hands on their hips and smiles on their faces they had already won the day, it did not matter if they could dance or not.

Unbelievably their little dance was perfect, it did not last long and they all finished together with a stamp kick. It is always important that you finish together.

The parents burst into applause, one dad shouted out "Yippee" another "Howdy" and they all joined in calling for "More, more".

That was the only dance they knew, so they did it over again. Jean was called for and praised for her patience. Grace and Flavia rushed from work in time to see them, Jean had said it would be good and it was.

'Better than any of your other classes' Grace told her with pride.

There was a call for further classes with older children who did gymnastics but indicated interest in line dancing. Jean took along recorded music for them, but still kept to the piano for the babies, as it had to be a slightly slower tempo.

Mr Digby praised her no end, confirming that it took a certain type of teaching, when confronted with the very young, he felt unable to do so. He was a good head teacher, very good at organizing the staff. He had an air of authority but the youngsters were not inspired by him they feared him.

Should a child be bad enough that sending it

to Mr Digby's office was called for you would think it was going to the gallows.

Many things were different at school now Jean very much doubted if Miss Collingwood would have agreed with line dancing and the dressing up that is probably why they have always ran round in rings.

After the rug episode, Jean never asked but looking at it wondered where it had been for all these years. They told her the value of it and that was not just because of the way it was made, but how and more important, when.

Some time ago and it could be Chinese.

She must ask Clive how he came by it. She never did ask, as she did not see much of him, apart from, sleeves rolled up spade in the air digging away at the top of Flay's garden.

Paul their son came for a brief visit, something to do with an empty wooden chest of Aunties he had his eye on. While considering and measuring this chest which in due course he thanked her for and took home. Jean had no use for it at all the age of the rug came to mind.

'Where did your father get that rug from?'

she asked Paul.

'That belonged to Lucy, she covered her rabbit's cage with it at night, dad found her a better one so she dumped the dragons.'

'Who?' Jean queried.

'Lucy'

'Well I am none the wiser, never heard of a Lucy who is she?'

'Oh didn't they tell you? You best ask Dad or Bobby' Paul realising that perhaps he had put his foot in it, tried to make a hasty retreat.

'No you wait up a bit young man I am asking you, who is Lucy?' He was not going to get out of this.

'Well, don't let on I told you, promise?'

'Yes carry on'

'Promise you will act surprised when they tell you and don't bring me into it.'

'I will be surprised'

'And you won't say I know' a worried Paul asked her.

'For Christ sake just get on with it and tell me who this dam Lucy is and why it is so secret,' she was shouting at him now.

'I can't tell you'

'You will bloody tell me' she dragged him into the kitchen and pushed him into a chair.

'Go' she waited for him to begin. He was like one of her kids at school she would like to send him to Mr Digby's office right now.

'You didn't promise.'

'I promise, cross my heart' He took a very deep breath while Jean waited, her hand on her heart and her head to one side staring at him waiting.

'She lives with dad' he blurted out.

'What in my house, and I never knew, what is the dirty cow doing in my house and in my bed as well I suppose.'

'Mum don't go calling her names, you don't know her.' Paul wishing he had not got into this, why didn't he just say I have no idea where the rug came from? Oh, he was going to be in trouble for this from someone.

'She must be a dirty cow to shack up with your dirty father and I've seen the state she let her rug get in.'

'Mum you promised remember please keep me out of this.'

'Wait until I see Clive.' She looked out the kitchen window and she could see him.

'In fact I will go and see him now'

'Mum stop, think about this, you left remember he is alone and does as he likes.'

'Are you taking sides?'

'No Mum, well maybe I am, at least wait until you can talk this over with Grace.' Knowing Grace would see the funny side of it and have a more sensible approach.

'I think I had better be off if you don't mind Mum, I will take the chest with me.'

'Yes go' she said to her son still looking out the window.

Within five minutes, Jean was marching up Flavia's garden to have a word or two with her husband.

'Oh hello' a surprised Clive said as he looked up when he see her coming.

'Who is this trollop you have shacked up with in my house?' started Jean. Clive feeling flustered with a lot of well, ums, wiped his nose on his cuff, looked Jean up and down, bracing himself he stood upright, stared at Jean as he said,

'Well' in a louder voice than he normally used, Clive told her.

'Jean it is nothing to do with you, as you walked out to live with your trollop I consider that house to be mine, and I do believe you told me so at the time. Lucy is a very good friend of mine, not a trollop at all.'

Lost for words after the initial onslaught, taken back as he called Grace a trollop, Grace would not like that at all. She made some sort of huffing noise and marched back up the garden.

Two minutes later, she was out again, dragging the rug.

'Give her this back' she yelled as she slung it to the ground outside the kitchen window. He did not touch the rug it he left it where she had tossed it on the ground.

Flavia saw it there when she arrived home from work, collecting it up returned it to Jean and Grace.

'What's this doing outside my kitchen window?'

'Where was it?' asked Grace. Jean did not speak.

'Give it here I will put it back.' Grace and Flavia returned the rug to the sitting room with raised eyebrows and "Oo-er" comments. Returning to the kitchen Grace spoke to Jean.

'Tell us then ducks' she said to Jean's back as she busied herself at the sink.

'Nothing to say just gave it back to where it

came from.'

'Hey, what has been going on here today?'

It was school holiday so Jean had what she considered her well, deserved rest. Upsets like this did not come into it.

Having time now, she reconsidered the situation, as she was getting over the shock. Perhaps he was right it was nothing to do with her. Grace was not a trollop though he could apologies for that.

She had never since she had known him, heard him raise his voice like that or care about anyone or thing so much.

Jean eventually answered Grace's question,

'School holiday yes great fun, teas ready' seeing she was not going to talk about it they said no more.

'We are painting tonight' said Flavia.

'More painting it is a never ending job.'

'Afraid so, Lucas has painted every ceiling that is a good thing over with, now we start on the doors, yuck, gloss paint, I am not very good at that, can't wait to start the walls.'

'It will not be long before you can move in.'

'I'm not sure it still looks an awful lot to do'

'Would you like me to call in decorators

love, get it over and done with?'

'No we want to do it ourselves.'

'What about curtains and drapes, shall I get our lady to measure up and you choose the fabric you like?'

'Oh no, I will make them myself' Grace looked at Jean with a, we will see look, but said

'Lovely darling'

'Are you taking the mickey Mum? I was very good at sewing lessons at school we had to learn all that sort of thing in our finishing year. And I can cook, better than you I'll let you know.'

'Ho miss hoity-toity private educated girl'

'You see we will invite you to dinner when we are settled.'

'Can't wait'

'What can't you wait for dinner or us to be settled?'

'Stop it you two,' shouted Jean. Just like her babies, they did as she told them, in case the Mr Digby threat cropped up again.

Chapter Nine

Tommy Albright continued to attend the six o'clock club, never learning very much apart from the enjoyable lesson he had with Flavia. Line dancing proved to be his forte, with much enthusiasm, he dressed perfectly for the part, cowboy boots, jeans and a Texan hat did wonders for him. One week he came along with a friend, Connie a skinny little thing with long straight hair almost to her bottom, glasses, pale skin, tiny hands and feet.

'And bad eyes sight' said Tracy.

'How do you know that?'

'She must have, not to care if she is seen with him.' Connie stayed close to Tommy, so close she appeared to be leaning on him.

He stood waiting for the class to begin, one hand in his back pocket and the other hand, thumb only in a front pocket. He had practiced this pose from a poster of James

Dean hanging on his bedroom wall. Not quite getting the look right but with practice he would, head down, hat back, eyes looking from under the brows. Oozing sex, he was doing that all right, just had to show it.

It was starting to work he had Connie's attention.

'Crikey have you seen what Tommy has brought along' Jean said to Grace, who had already met her at the door, where the pair of them had a dispute over who was going to pay to come in. In a posh voice, Connie told him she preferred to pay for herself and did so.

Nobody spoke to them, just stared, and they did not speak to each other, just stood waiting for Jean.

'Let's have a warm up to start, something you know, those who don't know it take a seat and watch,' meaning Connie, who still stood close to Tommy.

The music started, they quickly got in line. Jean stopped the music, and then restarted from the beginning calling out stamp, kick turn or whatever.

Little Connie did it perfectly with ease, just a tiny stamp and a neat turn, barely a kick more just a lifting of her foot.

Jean and Grace did a surprised eyebrows raise to each other.

The evening continued this way, there was not a line dance that Connie did not know. Everyone wanted to talk to her now.

'Yes I have done line dancing before,' was about her only comment. Tommy proudly stood there now with his arm around Connie's shoulders.

'Cocky arse' said Tracy 'wonder if she's as good at sex as she is at dancing?'

'Haven't seen him take a grab at her'

'Not much to grab, skinny tart.'

'You sound jealous'

'Come off it, anyone could have Tommy, all you'd have to say would be "oh yes" and he would be away, take us all on he would.'

'What one at a time or all together?'

'Whatever he'd try Miss as well'

'What about Grace?'

'Now there he would come up against it, he would try but I bet he wished he hadn't.'

All the girls who were chatting about Tommy laughed very loud. He looked away quite aware that he was the cause of their hilarity. Jean clapped,

'A new one now come along everyone form lines and follow me.' Grace fumbled a bit with this one and could see Connie was better than she was, thinking to herself,

'Shit I must practice more.'

There was to be a wedding!

Tommy and Connie were getting married, he did not want to get married just yet, but he had made her pregnant, therefore with his and her father threatening him, a rushed wedding was to take place.

'If you want us to get married, then we want a cracking wedding' he told their dads.

They invited everyone they knew. All the club members, Jean, Grace and Flavia's name was on their invite. Explaining to Connie about Lucas she agreed, yes him as well.

It was a large wedding, and to some standards, they would term it rough, but jolly and happy. Held at the local Catholic Church a long service, Grace moaned.

Afterwards a buffet, there were too many guests to sit down. They had a live band supplying the music and very good they were. There was not a time when the floor was not crowded with unruly dancers. Quite drunk and getting drunker by the minute.

There was a call for line dancing, so many rushed to the floor. The bride hoisted her wedding dress up and joined in with the guest.

'Come on Miss' called Tommy as he grabbed Jean by the hand and pulled her up to dance, Jean calling "Grace" for support, Grace followed. After much line dancing, Tommy grabbed the microphone and told everyone now my dancing teachers will demonstrate the samba.

'Will we?' said Jean.

'Not me' said Grace, both holding back.

'Go on you two they are all drunk anyway.' They cleared the floor, and Jean and Grace gave a fancy stepped demonstration of the samba. Followed with a call for more, with much shaking of their heads, they sat down.

'Who'd have thought that randy Tommy married' said Flavia.

'Do you think they will still come to the six o'clock club?'

'Don't see why not?'

'She's pregnant that's why not'

'Oh yes.'

She was right they did not come anymore. That is not until well over a year later, Tommy turned up on his own, drunk.

He moved among the dancers being a nuisance. Some were new and did not know who Tommy was others like Tracy could remember him well.

He still grabbed "bits of you" which was Grace's version of him trying a grope, now it appears he grabs bigger bits. A few squeals and an "Oi" coming from various girls, then a whack round the face from Tracy.

'Clear off Tommy you're a bleeding pig' she shouted 'tell him Miss.'

'Well, yes - Grace' Jean called. Grace was at the desk counting the money. She came in sharpish.

'Tommy, go home to your wife' she told him sternly.

'I left her' he said. A gasp went round 'left her and her screaming kid.' He sat down putting his head in his hands, looking far from leaving.

'He won't go, her brother will have him.'

'He had better go soon or her brother will more than have him.'

'Not in here he won't' said Jean. No sooner

were the words out of her mouth when, the door opened wide not quietly.

'Oh dear' said Jean 'er can I help you?' she addressed the two men who banged into their dance hall.

'It is five pounds each' said Grace stepping forward with her hand held out. Pushing her aside one of them asked,

'Is Tommy Albright here?' Ignoring Grace.

'There' said Tracy pointing to the heap still with his head in his hands.

'Excuse me' said one man, they grabbed Tommy, a shoulder each and with another 'excuse me' marched him out of the hall with everyone following and pushed him into a car.

'Never to be seen again' said Tracy as they drove away in a rush.

'Murdered and dumped'

'Surly not' said another.

'Be warned' Tracy grinned, waggling her finger at the boys.

Flavia amidst the painting received a phone call from her father.

'I think you should have said!' was how he began the conversation.

'Hello Daddy, how unusual for you to telephone me but how nice, of course.'

'You should have said.' He repeated,

'I did, hello Daddy, I said.'

'You should have told me who lives next door to you' his voice getting a little loud.

'Oh that, did I not say?'

'You know dam well you did not, I am just shocked and you not saying makes me more shocked, with you.'

'This does sound a bit of a stupid conversation Daddy, can you tell me why you are upset.' Now he was shouting at her,

'I just did' he almost screamed at her.

'Daddy you are obviously upset I will phone you back in an hour then we can talk properly.' She hung up on him.

'What is up' asked Lucas, putting down his paintbrush and looking at her face.

'It is dad he has found out who lives next door and is getting off on one. I never thought he would find out, I wonder how he did, and why he is so bothered.'

'Did he hang up on you?'

'No I told him I would telephone back later, he was shouting so.' Flavia did not return her father's phone call Lucas nagged her to do so.

'He was very good to us buying the house I think you should phone back with an explanation at least.'

'I can't it will make matters worse,'

'He will phone back you know.' A worried Lucas told her.

'I doubt it, I doubt if he will ever phone again.' She nonchalantly said with an air of indifference.

'Flay please think about this, it is your dad and your mum, oh heck try keeping it peaceful.' Lucas had a good relationship with his parents, they were a nice mum and dad, just as they should be, he found it most upsetting trying to imagine if his parents were separated it would be unbearable.

Huffing and sighing, looking at the face Lucas was pulling she could stand it no longer.

'I am going to see mum' and Flavia went next door to be in Grace's company.

After only five minutes, Lucas followed her,

'Did she tell you?'

'Tell me what? No I don't think she told me anything,' said Grace puzzled, looking at one then the other 'go on then tell me.'

'It's just dad phoned.'

'Oh I don't want to hear this' Grace looked disapprovingly at them and continued dusting the book shelves and studying the books she had taken out from the shelves.

'He is cross' said Lucas.

'So what's new?' she shrugged 'oh I get it, he has found out about me next door hasn't he?' she shrugged her shoulders again in so what manner and carried on with her books.

'Yes Mum afraid so and he is not a happy bunny, fairly shouting at me.'

'God Almighty that man, it's the double barreled name you know, makes him think he is above the rest of us. Don't let him worry you, I don't anymore and my life has been better for it' she continued with the books as Jean came in with a towel round her wet hair.

'Your life is better for what' she asked having heard the last remark.

'It is dad Jean he has found out mum lives next door and he was screaming at me down the phone. Flavia also started handling the books with interest, to put emphasis on not caring about dad.

Lucas looked strained.

'He has been very good to you both, I suppose he needs some reason his daughter is living so close to his ex-wife.'

'Exactly' said Lucas, 'I feel awkward Jean how will I feel next time we meet?'

'Maybe we won't meet again' Flavia mumbled into a book.

'Flay how unkind.' Mother and daughter paid more attention to the books, not caring about Lucas or Jean's opinion.

Suddenly Lucas stood up pointing to Flavia in a raised voice told her,

'You just go and telephone your father and stop acting like a spoilt brat, go now and phone him.' She banged the book down that she was holding, very well she would but he was to stay there.

'Whew that was brave' said Grace after she left to make the dreaded phone call.

'I say Chuck how masterful' giggled Jean.

'Well she asked for it.' Lucas sat down again relieved.

It was never discussed how the conversation went with father and daughter but before the week was out a cheque came in the post "to help with the interior of your house" and a short letter enclosed.

'What on earth did you say to him on the telephone, hope you didn't lie to your father, is he okay now?' asked Lucas.

'Yes fine was the only answer she gave me' he told Jean later 'it seems strange to me one minute furious with her the next sending more money.'

Jeremy was upset, things he had no control over always went against him.

His daughter who he longed to be a son was his first disappointment.

He loved Grace at one time, he thought her funny, she made him laugh, but he was sure he could tame her, turn her into the lady he needed her to be, befitting his wife. His next disappointment, it did not work and as she got older, she got worse and he had no control over her at all.

His daughter thankfully was the lady, or madam, whatever way you looked at it that he wanted his wife to be.

He could not send Grace to boarding school as much as he thought she needed to go, so he sent her packing. Got rid of her, told her to go and they would divorce. She did not seem to care. Immediately she went he was missing her or missing female company and made a point of looking out all the time for someone suitable.

His idea of 'suitable' changed daily and they grew younger. Divorced women were out, they were someone else's cast offs. No matter that is what he is. So not divorced meant unmarried therefore younger. At first, he liked his girlfriends to be young, they did as they were told, admired him, after Grace who was a bit of a know-all, these were the opposite, a little bit dim.

They knew nothing, then that began to get on his nerves, stupid and ignorant. They looked good, very attractive girls but no common sense. They had nothing of interest to say about anything, to him just down right boring.

He started to think that perhaps Grace was not so bad after all.

Along the grapevine came word to him that Grace was living with a woman. It all fitted into place the stubborn confidence she had with him. Had she always been a lesbian? Alternatively, was it something she turned into, or maybe she was just trying it?

He started to hate the mother of his child, he felt his life ruined because of her.

If only he had chosen someone different in the first place, someone accustomed to a higher class of living, maybe a frump as they all appeared to be but things would have been so much better.

Now Flavia who in his opinion he had done everything for was turning to her mother. He found it unbearable.

After Flavia's phone call when she assured him he came first even before Lucas, he was her beloved father, no other person would ever take his place he felt better.

Still deep down knowing he would not have had half the trouble if she had been the boy he wanted.

Flavia lied to her father.

All these matters turned Jeremy into a changed man. He was unhappy. He was becoming ill. He was still fit but did not feel it. Even with the loss of his hair, he was still smart, attractive to those who had not a hair fetish. "Bald of the head, good in the bed" a friend told him.

'Great expectations then I could be a

disappointment.'

'What sort of talk is that chum, cheer up.'

He became worse and felt miserable with no reason apart from depression.

To make things worse he wished to adjust his will. He is a very wealthy man a fine executive with many outlets throughout the United Kingdom and other countries. All managed by excellent staff. Still holding the controlling interest but did very little, compared with the early years.

A very nice lady solicitor advised him about the adjustments, while his secretary who he had taken along with him made notes. He made a further appointment with the solicitor alone, things he did not want to discuss in front of his secretary.

'You have a problem Mr Haden-Moore?' she asked him surprised that they had not covered what was essential during his first visit.

'Yes, first I am Jeremy and can I take you out for dinner tonight or any other night you prefer.' She was astounded, divorced and single, alone and always busy this did not happen to her often. She could not remember the last time she went out on a date.

'Why not? Tonight will be fine.' She said without having to give it much thought. Jeremy was pleased, she does not have a hair fetish, not until now realising how his baldness affected him, relieved Jeremy smiled. He was never concerned how the young girls he dated felt, all they could see was his money.

'Do you mind if I stay as I am? I have to work late it would not leave me much time to go home and change.'

'Not at all, you look nice as you are, you say a time.'

'Er I should be done by seven thirty. No I will be done by seven thirty.'

'Until then' said Jeremy leaving a lot bouncier than when he first arrived at her office.

This was just what he needed, Helen the solicitor's name, was in the same situation as he. Divorced a few years ago and since then just involved in her work.

'Have you any children' Jeremy asked her during the meal that evening.

'One son'

'I have one daughter, more trouble than sons.'

'Are they? Don't you be so sure.'

This was the first of many evenings they spent together progressing to weekends, many weekends, his place or her place, it did not matter and next the planning of a holiday together, that they both needed.

'Where shall we go?' asked Jeremy.

'A long way away, as far away as possible.'

'New Zealand is a long way away' casually Jeremy answered still thinking.

'There it is then' Helen grinned at him.

'Do you mean it?'

'Yes I do and make it for a considerable time.'

'Wow yes we will do it.' Jeremy's secretary made the necessary arrangements and they left leaving the secretary to tell the staff.

Flavia received just a brief note and of all things a blank cheque.

"I am going to New Zealand for a month or two, you can fill in any amount you need for the house while I am away, don't rob me! Love you Dad"

'Lucas do look, dad is off to of all places New Zealand'

'Well, well, wonder who he is going with?'

'You don't think he is going there alone, not

taking one of his bimbo's surely.'

'A blank cheque! Crikey he really is a nice man, to you at least.'

'He is getting better.'

Flavia did not rush to tell Grace there was no need, if the occasion did arise she would.

The occasion did arise

Flavia received further information from New Zealand after two months.

"I am staying longer probably for six months at least. Just to keep you informed I remarried last Saturday, to the friend I came with, Helen. I hope you like her I will send some photos when we get back from our honeymoon. Love from Dad."

'We must tell Grace now, you can't keep that a secret from your mum.'

Lucas and Flavia broke the news gently in case she felt the same as Jean did about Lucy. Apart from being surprised, she did not care and looked forward to the photos.

'Don't show her she is only being nosey' said Jean.

'I know I am, surely I can see the bimbo'
'No he will want to see a photo of me next'
'Oh he already has' said Flavia 'with Buster.'

'Why did you do that?' asked Grace, as Jean held her hands to her face in horror.

'Don't be daft he already knew about you, he just did not know you lived next door.'

'What photo did you show him?'

'This one I keep in my purse.' She produced a rather nice photo that she always kept with her of the two of them together looking very happy, along with a Buster who did not.

'What did he say?'

'Nothing much, he didn't like the cat.'

Grace huffed, never did like cats much.

Two or three weeks later, the photographs arrived.

'Look, look!' Flavia came rushing into the kitchen with them.

'Give us here, let's see. The photos Jean' Grace called out to her as she was upstairs.

'Wow look, she is not a bimbo, she is lovely'

'Yes he has done pretty well for himself considering his baldness' said Flavia.

'Your stepmother'

'Yes so she is' taking a closer look

'How old do you think?'

'About your age.'

'Youngish then!'

154

Chapter Ten

Brian Digby was a good head teacher, but did not like it at their school much, did not like the staff much either. They were all women the only male he spoke to all day was under eight. He found it hard trying to mix with the "petticoats" as he called them.

Jean he believed to be the best of the bunch. She liked him, starting to think more than she had liked Miss Collingwood, she and the last head had been great pals, but when it came to education he had a modern approach, Jean liked that. He had told all the teachers that before the beginning of next term, they would have a day's meeting as he had some sweeping changes to make.

This caused a commotion nobody liking the sound of that, Miss Atkins declared she would just sweep out of the door if he started on her.

The subject on her mind, and a few telephone calls from other colleagues objecting before they knew what it was about put Jean in a quandary. Determined to enjoy her holiday before next term and now she had this Clive business, she would draw the blind in the kitchen tomorrow and not look at him.

This she did, but she could hear him, whistling. Christ he sounds happy whatever is the matter with him, must be his bit, Jean mumbled to Buster, who betraying her went out his cat flap and joined Clive.

Bobby came to see Jean that afternoon, he was alone in the middle of the day, and not working Jean was pleasantly surprised.

'I didn't know you were on holiday'

'Just a few days Mum, I think perhaps I wish I was not, as I have the job here as a messenger.'

'Really, why so glum, what's up?'

'It is dad.'

'Oh him do not let him worry you, what is wrong with him now?'

'Well er, er'

'Yes get on with it.'

'He wants a divorce.'

'He wants what? No way, he is mad.'

'Divorce' she told Grace 'don't tell me he wants to marry that bit.'

'Darling don't upset yourself so, do you want him back?'

'No way, but asking me for a divorce, through our son as well. Why couldn't he ask me direct ashamed is he?'

'Didn't think you were talking to him?'

'I'm not' Jean did so much sighing and puffing that Grace thought her breathing will go out of rhythm in a minute and she will be hyperventilating.

'I'm going to bed'

'It is only seven thirty'

'Yes I know the time, I am having an early night' and off she went, she did not sleep she was still awake into the early hours of the morning, so much for an early night.

She remained in a mood for the rest of the week, unusual for Jean.

'Just down right grumpy' Grace told Flavia.

'I can't understand it, why should she care?' Bobby called to see her again, she kept out of his way, not quite refusing to see him, but when she see his car draw up she asked Grace to deal with him.

'I am taking a bath – a long one' and

marched off to the bathroom.

'She can't see you Bobby she is having a bath'

'I'll wait' he happily suggested as he settled in a chair.

'I wouldn't if I was you dear, she has a bad back' lied Grace 'and will soak for ages, resting afterwards.'

'I am sorry to hear that, poor mum, a hot bath is very good for easing backs. Did she say anything about dad?'

'Yes she did mention him he wants a divorce I understand.' Grace frowning at Bobby waited for his answer.

'Yes that's right they are not talking at the moment, not that dad is up on his words at the best of times, so this is why I have the job of relaying messages. I am not enjoying it one bit.'

'Does he plan on marrying again?'

'I don't know, he didn't say, I never thought about that, to Lucy you mean. He does think a lot of her, she is very nice.'

'You like her, does Pam?'

'Yes we all do, nothing to dislike about her, she is a bit scruffy I suppose, but then so it dad. She has animals.'

'Animals where are they?'

'All at dad's except her pony, her two rabbits, a lovely little dog and four cats are there.'

'My goodness four cats and a pony strewth, does Clive like animals?'

'Yes very much, mum wouldn't have any when she was at home, I always wanted a dog but no way.'

'Yes she is a bit like that wouldn't have Buster here if it wasn't for him taking us over, pushes himself on to people he does.'

'But I can't see what all this has to do with getting a divorce.'

'Shall I ask him?'

'No don't do that.'

Jean got less grumpy as she got accustomed to the request. Many early nights and bath soaks gave her time to think, she also agreed it was nothing to do with her anymore and a divorce would be best.

She told Grace who gave her a hug telling her she was a good girl.

Jean passed the message on to Bobby, upon telling his wife Pam she asked if he had mentioned their wedding to his mother.'

'No but she has a good idea, she can see no

other reason he would want a divorce now, which is fair enough.'

'Since Lucy agreed to marry your father he has been a different man,' said Pam.

'I know what did mum do to him to make him so withdrawn? She is nice though my mum, do you think so?'

'Yes a bit school teachery at times though, I wonder what she will be like with her grandchild when it gets here in April?'

'Just the same I guess, no she won't if we have a child she will love it, spoil it rotten, it must be clever like her and pretty like you, don't think she would take kindly to being called Grannie though.' He turned the pages of the newspaper he wasn't reading, looked over the top of his glasses at his wife,

'APRIL?' she nodded at him 'gets here in April what does that mean. Does it mean you are pregnant, I'm having a baby?' he excitedly stood up as the newspaper pages went in all directions he grabbed his wife.

'No dear it means I am having your baby, but you can have it if you think you can, I don't care'

'No thanks I'll have it when you have done the hard work ohhh, a baby for us.' They hugged and kissed with happiness.

They told Clive the divorce was to go ahead. Then told him their good news, Lucy was delighted for them.

'Another little animal to care for'

'Do you mind' said Pam, 'animal indeed.'

Then they collected a bottle of the best wine and went immediately to tell Jean and Grace.

Seeing the bottle Jean got the wrong idea

'If you think I am celebrating a divorce you are mistaken, however much you are pleased about it.'

'Mum sit down it is not that at all, we are going to be a family Pam is having my baby in April.'

'Our baby' said Pam.

Squeals with delight came from Grace.

'Putting a claim to it already, your baby indeed it will be ours, all of ours.' Jean cried silent tears of joy.

'A grandchild' she said to Grace that night.

'How long have they been married?'

'Eight, nine, could be ten years, I am not sure it seems a long while ago, given up on them, I thought they didn't want any children.'

'Hey Grannie'

'I know how long before Flavia starts, I don't think she will keep us waiting ten years. Then I'll be one as well, Grannie Lezzies that's us.' They laughed as they cuddled.

This is to be my first grandchild, no matter who follows this will be the first, so I shall buy all its firsts' she told Pam.

'What firsts Jean?'

'First shoes a must, first bed, first dress, coat or anything you are buying I will pay for it.'

'Thank you Jean that is most generous, you do understand it could be an awful lot.'

'Good, can we go shopping together?'

'Okay all the baby shops'

'Before you get too big, you won't want to go dragging round shops then.'

'Bobby is decorating our small bedroom turning it into a nursery.'

'I will buy the paint.'

'Jean, stop it.'

'Oh sorry am I taking over? Your mother, of course, I'm sorry we must consider her.'

'She will be glad you are buying, apart from not having much money, she already has nine grandchildren, not as excited as you, pleased for us, of course, but will not object to you buying things for one of her grandchildren.'

They went on their shopping trip, making a day of it, buying no end of baby goodies. Large items they were having delivered, like the cot.

They met one of Pam's friends she showed great interest in the baby shopping, stayed with them for a while helping them choose when they were uncertain. She told Pam she was sure it was a girl.

'So am I' said Jean.

'Don't get stuck on the idea, I don't want to disappoint you both'

After they parted, wishing each other farewell and good luck with the baby shopping, Jean said,

'She is nice, a friend of yours?'

'Don't you know who she is Jean?'

'Should I, never seen her before, a bit hippy but very pleasant, who is she?'

'That is Lucy, Clive's friend.' Jean nearly fell down with shock she wobbled a bit and put her hand on the nearest wall.

'You could have warned me.'

'How could I do that an introduction wasn't quite in order.'

'Do you think she knows who I am?'

'Yes, you did say your first grandchild, that didn't take much working out, therefore you had to be my mum or Bobby's and she knows my mother is already a grandmother.' They walked on in silence.

'She seemed very nice'

'She is'

'A lot younger than me'

'She is'

'Do you think she is a hippy?'

'She is'

'For goodness sake Pamela say something else besides - She is.'

'Okay Miss, she's nice, I like her, so does Clive and you did just then. It is just a shock for you to take in but she could be a lot worse, or nobody at all and Clive a lot worse, back to his old self.'

'You are right, just a shock, will she be a grannie too?'

'No but she will be married to grandad one day.' Jean grabbed hold of Pam's arm and started striding off dragging her along.

'Time for a cuppa, and a cream cake'

'Yes lets'

As they sat together drinking coffee and

eating very large cream cakes, Jean asked Pam 'Do you think they will get married?'

'Yes I think they intend to marry as soon as you and Clive are divorced.' Jean sat in silence looking at the shoppers passing by.

'You look upset Jean'

'Just a little sad.

Chapter Eleven

As Pam and Bobby had waited so long for this baby, they took no chances and Pam stopped working, she stayed at home enjoying a life of leisure, waiting. Time was drawing close, now they were into April and after one Sunday lunch with Jean and Grace, Paul and his wife were there as well, they started to discuss baby names.

'We still haven't chosen names' said Pam.

'It will be a girl' Jean was so sure, starting all of them of calling out girls names, Paul threw in Lucy without thinking.

'It is a nice name' said Paul as they all objected 'well I like it'.

'So is Jean nice'

'Who wants to be named after their grandmother, come off it' said Grace. This was how the name choosing went until Pam had her baby boy.

'Thank goodness it's a boy.'

'Mitchell, nice, they will call him Mitch'

The baby was born healthy, not too large, long legs.

'He is going to be tall' said Jean poking his legs, and feeling his feet.

'He is a bit noisy' Grace moaned.

'Not really, babies can be vocal'

'Bet he never stops, he'll be sent to Mr Digby's office more often than not, talking in class you mark my words.'

They did not know at the time that no child would they send to Mr Digby again.

Vicky Paul's wife, Jean's other son, was a hairdresser, Paul a plumber, water engineer she called him. They met when he came to install new sinks where she was working.

All the girls were attracted to him, he was rather good looking, and did have the habit of striping to the waist when working as he often got wet working in awkward places with water.

Just having a workman in the salon for a few days was enough to put the girls in a tizz. He was the silent type, like his dad. Vicky paid him the least attention, so he found her the most interesting and to the other girls surprise and disapproval, he asked Vicky for a date.

It moved on from there into romance and no sooner had Bobby married when Paul thought that is what he should do. In the same year, both brothers were married.

Nice girls, Jean always got on with them, having Vicky the hairdresser in the family was an asset. Jean never went to another hairdresser again, Vicky came to her house, it was more relaxed for them while she attended to Jean she would look at Clive's head wishing she could get her hands on his hair.

Unlike Jeremy who had lost his, Clive's hair had turned grey and appeared to grow more he was never going to go bald and by the look of it never going to have a haircut. He would put his hat on when he see Vicky giving his hair and eager look.

No babies came along so Vicky kept working and saving.

'I want my own salon' she told Paul.

'Yes dear, we all want things that we can't have.'

'Will you look at this?' she shoved her building society savings book across the table at him. Slowly taking a puzzled look inside, gazing up at his wife. Then turning pages, he sees the balance.

'Where did you get all this?' he asked.

'I saved'

'Saved from what?'

'My salary and tips, they mount up and any more I had over I put in there.'

'What for? Why didn't we spend it?'

'It is for my salon, you didn't go without, it was extra we would have wasted it.'

'You are serious aren't you, have you given this much thought?'

'No end of thought, you could say that is all I think about. At work all day I say to myself if this was mine I would do this or change that, it is not just a whim Paul.'

'You never said'

'No, until now I have been frightened to put it into words.' They discussed the possibilities all evening resulting in two ways to go, buy a going concern, and pay someone for their goodwill, but that could leave with the present owner. Alternatively, start afresh, make a shop, and turn suitable premises into a hairdressers.

Acquire a lease, make changes or open a new salon. This is what they did. What was on offer was either badly run down or in the wrong place, and all the best places were too expensive.

Vicky did not want to travel far as that would be wasted time, so they kept looking locally. Vicky's mother also a Victoria but never called Vicky showed great interest and was helpful. She was no hairdresser but excellent at paperwork and cleaning, she would turn her hand to most things.

Arriving at Vicky's place of work one day her mother whispered to Vicky as she was working on a client's hair,

'I must see you, take a break when you can I will wait in the charity shop next door.' It took Vicky less than fifteen minutes to find a moment to meet her mother next door.

'Whatever is the matter?'

'I have found your shop'

'Where?'

'The top of Richmond Road, where your father-in-law lives, it is on the corner. The people have done a runner and it is empty. I had a look inside, as the door was open, I asked a man there, he said they went bust and the lease would be coming up for renewal, what do you think.

'I know where you mean, they sold novelties, Christmas decorations.'

'Yes okay for Christmas but no good after, haven't sold a thing since, so got out, owing money, I guess.'

'Mum it would make a good hairdressers'

'It would love it is a large shop, double windows, door on the corner with a window either side. It is nice and clean, got a little kitchen at the back and most important a toilet. Lock up just what you want and plenty of parking for you clients.'

'I have to see this Mum, I will tell Sheila something has come up and I have to leave early.' In no time they drove to the shop in question, in the window now was a sign, lease to let. Making notes of the people involved, they paid them a visit.

Only half an hour later, they returned home owning a shop lease.

'Wait until we tell Paul.'

'No thanks, you tell him on you own' said Victoria I am off, phone me let me know what he says, don't blame me if he is cross.'

Paul was no problem, he liked the idea and they took a walk to look at the shop. They could walk it was that close.

'How many sinks will you need' he asked working out the pipe work in his head. 'I can see a boiler of sorts in the back there' just visible was the outer rooms.

'We must get the keys tomorrow and take a good look' they went home pleased with the idea and spent all evening drawing plans for sinks and all possibilities.

In less than a month, he had transformed the place into Vee's Salon. At one time, it was to be Vicky's, but changing her mind, she liked just Vee. Paul did all the fitting, plumbing and decorating, helped by colleagues and friends.

The theme was pink and blue, open corner windows with just draped side nets giving some privacy but allowing future clients to see inside. An announcement followed placed in the window regarding opening day, the same also advertised in the local newspapers. Appointments made before they were open.

Victoria helped Vicky most thought she was the owner they, were soon to be put right. Vicky also had two assistants a stylist and a junior girl learning the trade.

Jean had little to do with the proceedings and when she asked Clive, he was not at all sure. Paul was too busy and never seen by the family. Bobby helped him with the menial tasks, but was unable to report to his mother how good it looked.

Opening evening they were all there, family and friends came along. They could see what a good salon it was going to be.

Jean made an appointment noticing several pages were full and many pages turned before they could fit her in.

The salon was a success, Vicky and Victoria became well known and liked.

After Jean left home, they often see Clive scuffling past their shop window, which was on the corner of his road, as he went on the way to the supermarket.

Victoria had no husband and she was an awful flirt. After Clive made a journey to the shops she waited for his return, first waving and smiling, he also waved in return but looked a little embarrassed because of the women in the shop.

Victoria took to running outside to chat to him. One time she walked along the road with him, Vicky went out to see where they had gone. Her mother walked him to his house and went inside.

'What are you up to Mum? That is Paul's dad.'

'I know just being friendly'

'Can't you be friendly without running after him?' Victoria went back behind the desk as the telephone was ringing.

Two days later, they all looked up as a little tapping came on the window. It was Clive, making hand instructions to Victoria.

'Cover the phone dear, I am going out for a while' and she left Vicky staring with her mouth open, as her mother rushed out and went off with Clive.

No one ever got to the bottom of the 'goings on' as Paul called them.

'Your mother honestly she chases any man. I am sorry to say this about her but it is true. No wonder your father left her.'

'It was a long time ago Paul, I have no idea why my father left her, as she has never talked about it I guess it was her fault, and the way she flirts I am not surprised. I cannot remember her being any different. I am sorry but at the present, she seems to have her eyes set on your father, not a good idea, I keep telling her. Don't let Jean find out' worried Vicky.

Victoria was a smart woman small and neat, not at all the type you would expect to be attracted to Clive. Nothing was moving fast enough for her where Clive was concerned, so there was always Tosh, he was their window cleaner. Before he started work, Victoria made him a drink and much to Vicky's annoyance he spent more time talking to her mother than he did cleaning their windows.

Clive soon became fed-up with Victoria and tried to avoid her, he was beginning to find her attention a bit over powering. He took to walking the other way to the shops, going a longer way round so he did not pass Vee's Salon. It took him longer, but he did not have to put up with Victoria's chat, so he did not mind.

It was a pleasant walk past the recreation ground and Coal Meadow, which was just a rough piece of land with a few horses and a donkey grazing on it, belonging to goodness knows whom.

Passing by one day, he noticed a small horse had its feet stuck in some brambles and a young woman was trying to calm him while she released his legs. As she was having trouble, Clive went through the gate to help her with the brambles.

'Hold him' he said to her as he took out a pair of secateurs that were always in his pocket along with other useful items and started to snip the brambles from the animals feet, he kicked out a bit, but Clive was not bothered and soon had him free.

Looking at his legs the women decided he should have antiseptic cream applied as he had several skin tears.

'I live just over there, could you hold him still while I run and get it?' Off she went as Clive talked to the pony, which was much calmer now he slowly walked him away from the brambles. When the woman came back, apologising to Clive she introduced herself properly.

'Next time I am passing I will cut back these brambles of the floor it won't take a minute' Looking at the brambles, they could see it was difficult for the horses not to tread on them as they were creeping across the grass. The pony after his treatment, trotted off none the worse.

'Would you like a cup of tea, that is the least I can do, I am so grateful.' Not to be rude and liking the idea Clive accepted.

This was his first meeting with Lucy.

A closer look he could see she was a little older that he first thought. She lived alone with many animals.

'I lived with a bloke for three years, then he said the animals go or I go' she laughed 'what an compromise, you go mate, now, I told him and it's been me and them ever since.'

Walking back home Clive forgot about Victoria and after doing his shopping went the wrong way back, as he walked past the salon, out she popped as quick as lightening.

'Clive darling I have not seen you for ages, not unwell I hope?' she gushed over him.

'No,no,no,no,' Christ how many no's had he just said, he winced inwardly, lost for words, that was all he said.

She tucked her arm in his and accompanied him home, with Vicky objecting as her mother made off leaving an empty desk without any by your leave.

She soon came back as Clive made some excuse and she could tell she was not welcome.

'Oh back are you' said Vicky

'Yes was not long was I did you miss me?' One of the clients said,

'We see you go off with that dirty old Clive Mason, keep away from him if I was you, his wife had enough of him, left him for a woman, he put her off men for life,' she announced to everyone in the shop.

Oh thought Vicky, she does not know she is talking about my husband's parents. Some in the shop did, the silence was embarrassing and the matter dropped as the junior, Katy chimed in with,

'I think Mrs Preston should come out now Vick,' with a worried look.

'My God yes straight away.' Mrs Preston was having highlights to her hair and sat under heat for them to develop. All attention went on to Mrs Preston who fortunately had no idea that she had extra time and thankfully of no dire consequences.

'See the trouble you cause mother' Vicky said after they closed the shop 'people do notice, keep away from Clive.'

'I don't see why I should it is nothing to do with any of them.'

'Mum its Paul's dad for God sake.'

Clive could not have another encounter with Victoria she drove him up the wall. Good job he did not hear the conversation in the salon.

He always now, went and came back the long way round, besides he could see the pony and hopefully Lucy.

He did go back to Coal Meadow and clipped back all the brambles along the edge of the field as he promised. It took him some time, the horses gathered round watching him.

Then to his surprise, Lucy arrived holding two cups of coffee, as he was chipping the side near her house.

'Hello Clive' she said as she pulled out from her pocket a packet of biscuits and two carrots for Kite her pony. They sat on a mound of grass in the warm sun drinking.

'That's a funny name for a horse.'

'Pony' said Lucy.

'Whatever.'

'A bit embarrassing really I called him Kitty because I thought he was a girl, until someone pointed out to me the difference, which is very noticeable isn't it, not like cats where you have to take a good look. I felt such a fool, by then he got use to me calling him Kitty so I changed it to Kity, now it is just Kite. He doesn't mind comes to me whatever I call him. Daft aren't I?' Clive laughed a thing he seldom did.

'Clive I must repay you for your kindness, this is the council's job, trimming the hedges they charge us for grazing our animals here so they should keep it safe.

I would like to cook you a meal tomorrow, can you manage that, I am a good cook and always eat alone, do come and share with me.'

'Thank you, I will, all I ever have is ready cooked or take away I can't cook at all.'

'Right, good, seven o'clock, no six thirty for a glass of wine'

'Fine I will bring that'

'Don't dress up Clive come as you are with an empty tummy. I must get back to my washing machine, it should be finished now.'

'And I have a field to finish, tomorrow then' he called as she ran off to her washing machine.

That put a smile on his face for the rest of the day, and after his enjoyable evening with Lucy the next day, a smile for the rest of the week. They did enjoy each other's company

Clive had never talked to anyone as much as he talked to Lucy. Never feeling so relaxed or at ease with anyone before.

He in return invited her to his place, to see his large garden, explaining how he is a gardener but has lost interest.

During the evening meal they had together, they both confided their life history.

Lucy told him how she rented her house by Coal Meadow, excellent for Kite, it seemed a good idea to rent at the time but she has regretted it often. Her parents left her their house when they passed on but she did not want to live in it. She thought about buying another house then she decided to keep the money, she had never had any money to talk of and decided to rent.

As property prices have risen it was not such a good move, but she still has enough money not to work and to care for her animals that was ideal for her, and pay her landlord the rent he asked.

They were a strange pair to look at, scruffy looking, old clothes, they did not smell as people expected they would, perhaps Clive did some days when he forgot to wash. They were so alike they did not notice their appearance. They both liked their food and spent time planning their next meal. Lucy did the cooking and Clive the paying and often shopping with a list that Lucy provided for their next meal.

They made a point of seeing each other every day becoming grand companions. One day walking past the salon with Lucy and her little dog, Victoria rushed out the shop door to take a better look. They did not notice her.

'Did you see that?' she reported to Vicky, who was busy administering a perm to a client head and not gazing out the window.

'No Mum I didn't see anything'

'I am telling Paul' Victoria said as she shifted papers on the desk with gusto.

'You do that Mum' said Vicky not having a clue what she was on about.

'Who is this woman your mother is talking about?' asked Paul of his wife.

'I did not see a woman, does it matter if he is talking to someone?'

'Well no, but he hardly talks to us, let us face it' her husband puzzled who it was.

'Good job he has someone to talk to then.'

'I'll call in and see him'
'Paul for goodness sake, leave him alone.'

When Paul did go to see his father Lucy was there. He thought she was pleasant and friendly and his father happy, something he had not seen for a long time. Making Paul wonder what was happening.

She was a bit scruffy but he did not notice as she stood next to Clive in his untidy home, she fitted in, Paul felt the odd one out.

They kept this information to themselves and Victoria was under threat not to breathe a word to anyone, it was none of her business.

Lucy and all her animals moved in with Clive, some problem with her rented house brought that about, the landlord taking objection to her animals suddenly, she had an understanding with him before she accepted to rent his house.

'Maybe it was an interfering neighbour' suggested Clive.

Moving into Clive's house was to be just a temporary arrangement, but they both liked it. Clive deciding, finally, to rid the place of Jean's things, he very quickly had a ruthless clear out, making room for Lucy, four cats and a little dog. In his small extension, two rabbit.

He laughed out loud he was getting use to this laughing since he had met Lucy, all these animals, the house came alive. Cats were everywhere always finding one on his lap if he sat down for a second.

Bobby called to see his dad, also to meet Lucy, Pam approved, making great friends with Lucy immediately.

When she moved in with Clive, they all agreed not to tell Jean, she would find out eventually but not to go out of the way to tell her.

If it had not been for the dragon rug episode, when would she have found out? Now a divorce, things were moving on.

Trying to avoid Victoria had certainly changed Clive's life, what were the chances of passing the field just when Kite had his feet tangled and Lucy needing help. Clive pondered on this and still did not believe his luck.

Victoria was to remain….

'Insulted' she told Vicky, 'choosing that scruff over me.' She was stuck with the window cleaner; whom she found out was married to his third wife. She kept a watchful eye for any other man she could flirt with, suggesting to Vicky she had room to install a man's side to her business.

'I don't think so Mum, I don't do men's hair and they may want a shave'

'Oh I could do that.'

'Mum!'

Chapter Twelve

The divorce eventually settled, Jean's boys and their wives also Flavia and Lucas, Clive invited to his wedding, and that was all, it took place directly.

A small wedding, no fuss, quiet but so pretty. The bride and groom looking younger than their years, they were happy and in love.

They were clean, very clean for them. Clive's boys had never seen him so smart. Lucy wore, still hippy clothes, but a pretty, cream long dress with much lace, flowers in her hair, and she carried a single rose, that she gave to Clive as she got to the altar, they both held it throughout the service.

No one gave her away she walked down the aisle alone, as Clive stood alone, with no best man. They had a church wedding in a small chapel that Lucy attended.

After the service they went to Bobby and Pam's house for a meal that Pam's friend had kindly prepared for them, she also cared for baby Mitchell who was growing fast and enjoying the attention given to him while they enjoyed the celebration.

Grace took Jean to Paris for the weekend. Keeping well away from the wedding and enjoying a short break to take Jean's mind of the proceedings.

'We could get married' Grace told her as she sat wistfully gazing at nothing.

'You must be joking, two women only marry if they are lesbians and you are not one of those for Christ sake.' They laughed at the thought.

'I'll take that as a no, then.'

'Yes I will marry you, but no thanks.'

'I hope he stays happy now, as happy as us'

'He called you a trollop'

'Really, great I have always wanted to be a trollop, suppose we both are.'

'You're late ducks, something come up?' said Grace as she stirred the spaghetti bolognese she was making for their tea.

'You could say that,' Jean calmly said as she removed her coat.

'I think we will go to the cinema tonight' said Flavia 'there is a good film on in town, do you mind if I give tea a miss and grab a take away of sorts on the way.' She folded the newspaper she was reading.

She was still living with Grace and Jean but planning to move into their house next month, perhaps.

Flavia and Lucas were no bother to them they were used to having them around and would miss them when they did consider the house finished. Jean admitted it did look beautiful and it will be a shame to live in it, shame to cook in that ultra-modern kitchen.

'Okay none for you' said Grace, Flavia moved upstairs to get ready. Jean sat in her seat with a huge sigh.

'As bad as that, spill the beans, what disaster has happened at Victoria First School?'

'Mr Digby, as from now, has resigned.'

'NO, he can't do that in the middle of term.'

It is frowned on, apart from serious illnesses.

'He is ill is he, how serious?' Enquired Grace as if she cared, still stirring their dinner.

Poor Brian Digby he really was a nice bloke but no one cared about him, the rest of the teaching staff were glad to see the back of him.

'No not ill at all, fed up with teaching baby brats, his words, he is going to France teaching English to adults he has to go immediately to get the post. There will be a loss of salary this month's at least and may have to pay compensation for not giving notice.'

'Wow that'll teach him, ha pun, teach the teacher' Grace still stirred her food.

'Then I got a phone call,' she gave a long pause 'from the education department at your place, asking me to come for an interview immediately I finished school for the day.'

'My place? What at the Hall? I didn't know we had an education department'

'It's just an office, couldn't really call it a department but they do.'

'I didn't see you there, did you see me in my cupboard'

'No, I would have said hello if I did.'

'Who did you see?'

'Alan Clark'

'Never heard of him'

'And a governor, Conrad Knight'

'Him, oh yes I remember him with the young blond bit in the "Beef and Pork" restaurant that time.' Starting to talk quickly Jean said,

'As it was only last year, and I was second choice they were pleased to offer me the Headship and I am to start immediately not wait until next term.' Hyperventilating she grinned at Graces back as she was still stirred the food in the saucepan.

Turning slowly to face Jean after a pause, she said

'Well I hope you told them to stuff it.'

'Darling you know I didn't, AND'

'There is an And?'

'And, they are contemplating, well almost certain, next year they want to combine the infant school with the junior school. It will only need one head teacher. They prefer the infant school head teacher to take over, as it is not easy for junior school heads to adjust. First year children, need a different type of teaching, as they are such babies and I...'

'Stop, stop you have accepted and next year you will be head mistress of both schools' Grace squealed with delight, pulled Jean from her chair and whirled her round and round.

'I will be living with a Head Mistress after all, a very Big Head Mistress.'

'No dear a head mistress of a very big school.' Grace squealed again.

Flavia opened the door to say she was going

'What on earth are you two doing? No, don't tell me, call yourself a teacher you act like a pair of kids at times, and I can smell something burning. Goodbye.' She quietly closed the door leaving them alone.

Also by Mo Lily

Turning
This is my Turn
A Pint and a Push
A Port and a Push
Just the Ticket
Rat-arsed
Lad's at Forty
Single Mums – Gawd Bless 'Em
Partners even when we Dance

Turning

'Michael please don't do this, not here' were almost the only words his wife had said to him all evening, now she was pleading with him 'Stop please; I know you are not drunk, why are you acting this way? Take me home.'

This is my Turn

The new mini car, cream with a black roof and tinted windows, came over the bridge at probably a too fast a speed, turning left taking the road that ran along the quay.   Driving was Sandra Ross she had just moved to Clysworth in Cornwall from London

A Pint and a Push

'Tell them I fell off the bus coming home and I'm not going back' yelled Alan Phillips to his wife from upstairs. She stood in the hall with the telephone in her hand.

'Surely you can go back for one more week?' she called back upstairs to him.

'I'm not, so there, phone 'em, go on'

A Port and a Push

'I think we should get back to basics' said Whitey Philpott to his friends.

'Who do you think you are a prime minster?'

'What's a prime minster got to do with anything?'

'A prime minster said that.'

'Said what?'

'Back to basics'

'I don't remember that'

'On your bike one said'

Just the Ticket

Honk! Honk! Honk! The noise of a car horn repeatedly blasting on a quiet Saturday afternoon was disturbing.

'Who's making all that noise?' called Mrs Jasmine Collins from the kitchen, then looking out the window she saw who it was.

'It's that Kevin, what's wrong with him now?'

Rat-Arsed

When Hannah stood up she had the rat held by the tail between her thumb and first finger, her teeth were clenched together and her eyes half shut, her young sister Susie shouted

'Is it dead?'

'Yes, well and truly, get out of the way'

Lad's at Forty

It was the day I killed the cat, I did not mean to kill it, and it was my cat, not that it gave me the right to take its life.

Why all the fuss from others who did not like the cat anyway. I was the one upset

Single Mum's Gawd Bless 'Em

I quickly pulled my knickers back on, peeing in the bushes, in the dark was not pleasant. Sarah called out to me,

'Hurry up' she tooted on her car horn, that's it draw attention to ourselves. My four-inch heels kept sinking into the mud and long grass. I scrambled back into her minuscule wreck of a car

About the Author

Mo Lily lives in Dorset England with her husband
and two elderly cats.
The beautiful South Coast is in close proximity.

She was born in London's East End and although
she has lived in Dorset for many years, still
considers herself an East Ender.

As she is profoundly deaf, the written word is very
important to her, television subtitles, telephone
text and of course books.

Printed in Germany
by Amazon Distribution
GmbH, Leipzig